# Warmth and Darkness

★ **A Strange Space™ Novella** ★

## KATIE SILVERWINGS

*Memphis, TN*

PepTalk Productions, LLC

Publisher's Cataloging-in-Publication Data
provided by Five Rainbows Cataloging Services

Names: Silverwings, Katie, 1991- author.
Title: Warmth and darkness : a Strange Space novella / Katie Silverwings.
Description: Memphis, TN : PepTalk Productions, 2024. | Series: Strange Space novella, bk. 5.
Identifiers: LCCN 2023922526 (print) | ISBN 978-1-959922-09-4 (paperback) | ISBN 978-1-959922-10-0 (hardcover) | ISBN 978-1-959922-11-7 (ebook) | ISBN 978-1-959922-12-4 (audiobook)
Subjects: LCSH: Extraterrestrial beings--Fiction. | Family--Fiction. | Outer space--Fiction. | Science fiction. | Illustrated works. | BISAC: FICTION / Science Fiction / Space Exploration. | FICTION / Science Fiction / Alien Contact. | GSAFD: Science fiction.
Classification: LCC PS3619.I58 Wa 2024 (print) | LCC PS3619.I58 (ebook) | DDC 813/.6--dc23.

Published by PepTalk Productions, LLC  2024
Memphis, Tennessee, USA
www.PepTalkProductionsLLC.com

# Books by Katie Silverwings

## FEATHERED FRIENDSHIP
★ A Strange Space™ Novella ★

## CELADON
★ A Strange Space™ Novel ★

## HOW OCEAN MERLANI STOLE THEIR NAVIGATOR
★ A Strange Space™ Novel ★

## THE GARDEN IN THE DARKNESS
★ A Strange Space™ Novel ★

## WARMTH AND DARKNESS
★ A Strange Space™ Novella ★

Available now on Amazon and Barnes & Noble and at
**www.KatieSilverwings.com**

The printing of this edition of *Warmth and Darkness* was made possible through the generous support of the members of the Strange Space™ Fan Club, including:

## Astral Navigator

Sharon T. Hinton

## Space Adventurer (1 Year)

Tabitha

Thank you so much to all of my Fan Club members and supporters! I couldn't do this without you.

To find out more about the Strange Space™ Fan Club and join for free, visit:

www.KatieSilverwings.com/Fan-Club

# Characters Appearing in this Story

The following list of characters is divided by species and arranged in order of their appearance in the narrative. Only characters with significant "speaking roles" have been detailed here. Characters who are mentioned but do not appear are not included. Listed family connections are not exhaustive.

### *Florivans*

**ELDER CELADON TOREVAL**

They/them. Also known as "Dons," "Val," or "Donnie." Primary Quantum Space Drive Engineer, SCV *Aegolius*. Youngest of the Florivan Council of Elders; Defense Fleet Elder. Counterpart to **Lt. Hsu Li.** Adoptive entile of **Mirawynd** and heart's-sibling to **Elias Rudolph**.

**MIRAWYND**

They/them. Also known as "Wyndi." An orphaned survivor-smallest kitten. Second Darter Squadron mascot. Counterpart and ward of **Julian Potts**. Great-grandkitten of **Elder Marine**.

**RANGER CAPTAIN AQUA NEYRIL**

They/them. Primary Quantum Space Drive Engineer, LSRV *Bee*. Counterpart to **Ranger Captain Marilyn O'Connor**.

**ELDER AZUL MYRNAI**

They/them. Primary Quantum Space Drive Engineer, LSS *Caleana Major*. Counterpart to **Rebecca Montgomery**.

### *Humans*

#### ADMIRAL JENNIFER MARVIN

She/her. Also known as "Jenny". Head of the Sol Coalition Defense Fleet. Commanding officer of SCV *Aegolius.*

#### PETTY OFFICER 3RD CLASS ELIAS RUDOLPH

He/him. Also known as "Rudy." Darter Maintenance Technician, 2nd Darter Squadron, assigned to SCV *Surnia.* Boyfriend of **Hsu Li** and heart's-brother of **Celadon Toreval**.

#### LT. HSU LI

He/him. Lead Astral Navigator, SCV *Aegolius.* Former personal assistant to **Admiral Marvin.** Called "Beacon" by Florivans generally and "Sunshine" by **Elder Azul.** Boyfriend of **Elias Rudolph** and counterpart to **Elder Celadon**.

#### MS. HARRINGTON

She/her. An officer of the Sol Coalition Diplomatic Corps, temporarily assigned to SCV *Aegolius.*

#### PILOT-SERGEANT JULIAN POTTS

He/him. Also known as "Sarge." Second Darter Squadron pilot, assigned to SCV *Surnia.* Counterpart and guardian to **Mirawynd**.

#### PILOT-COLONEL GUNTHER HANNEMANN

He/him. Commanding officer of the First Darter Squadron, assigned to SCV *Aegolius.* Former head test pilot of Project Snail Darter.

#### OTHER HUMANS APPEARING

Ensign Phoenix, Dr. Dupree.

## *T'irsh-fel*

### ATTENDANT RYZYK

She/her. Red feather ruff. A junior member of the crew of the T'irsh-fel battle cruiser *Swift Justice*.

### PILOT ZYRR

He/him. Orange feather ruff. A shuttle pilot and member of the crew of the T'irsh-fel battle cruiser *Swift Justice.*

### HIGH COMMANDER QZVYR

He/him. Purple feather ruff. A high-ranking officer of the T'irsh-fel hierarchy, commanding officer of the battle cruiser *Swift Justice.*

# CONTENTS


Characters Appearing in this Story ⋯⋯ ix

1 ⋯⋯ 1

2 ⋯⋯ 18

3 ⋯⋯ 29

4 ⋯⋯ 44

5 ⋯⋯ 57

6 ⋯⋯ 65

7 ⋯⋯ 75

8 ⋯⋯ 86

9 ⋯⋯ 96

10 ⋯⋯ 105

11 ⋯⋯ 114

12 ⋯⋯ 124

13 ⋯⋯ 132

14 ⋯⋯ 136

15 ⋯⋯ 144


## Appendix


Timeline of *Strange Space™ Adventures* ⋯ 158

On the T'irsh-fel ⋯⋯ 160

On Florivan Biology and Culture ⋯⋯ 163

On Character Identities and Pronouns ⋯⋯ 168

# Warmth and Darkness

★ A Strange Space™ Novella ★

# KATIE SILVERWINGS

"Remind me, Jenny..." Celadon Toreval begins, wrapping their lower pair of arms a little tighter around their torso to hold in a shiver. "*How* many more days of this do we have left?"

Jenny Marvin, the russet-skinned human walking beside Toreval along the corridor leading from SCV *Aegolius'* main shuttle bay, looks down to them and chuckles lightly. The movement makes her thick bun of tawny curls threaten to escape the long brass hairpins holding it all in place at the base of her neck. "Five or six, if all goes well."

"Oh, is that all?" One of Toreval's large catlike ears twitches as they turn all three of their large golden eyes up to meet hers. They're used to having to look up to carry on a conversation; humans on average are at least a head taller than any Florivan. Toreval themself is on the short end for their species, too, while Jenny is tall for hers. "Here I thought we'd been in these talks for weeks already."

"It's only been twelve hours, by my count." Jenny laughs again and unzips her long insulated coat while she walks, exposing the rest of her ivory-trimmed dark green dress uniform and the Fleet Admiral's insignia on her collar. "What, Celadon," she teases, "don't tell me you're finally starting to regret throwing your lot in with me."

"Oh, no, nothing like that. Never." Toreval keeps all four arms wrapped tightly around their body. They're not nearly warm enough yet to shed their own matching coat. Underneath, not that anyone has actually *seen* it today, they're wearing the same sort of dress uniform as Jenny—albeit adapted to accommodate their additional set of arms and long prehensile tail. Their silver hair is held in a set of loose looped braids that are tucked up behind their ears in a bun with a carved wooden ring and pin, and they wouldn't be surprised if there are icicles hanging off of it after the day they've had. The veil-like tails of the wide green and ivory Elder's ribbons they wear twined through their braids were frozen stiff the last time they checked.

"Good," Jenny replies, still with a trace of wry humor in her voice, "because I suspect the day you give up on me and go back to Procyon is the day I lose the rest of my jumpers too."

"Oh," Toreval teases back, "I doubt *all* of the volunteers would follow me..." They gesture vaguely with one of their pale greenish-blue hands before tucking it back into the relative warmth of their coat. "I rather think they like working for you."

"You don't give yourself enough credit, *Youngest*," Jenny tells them. She does a passable imitation of the tone the older members of the Council usually use when addressing Toreval by their title. "It's *you* they've followed this far, and we both know it."

"We have as much at stake as you do," Toreval says absently, even though they know Jenny of all people is aware of that. "My people threw our lot in with humanity the day we gave you the Drive and started jumping your ships through the Strange. If you fall, we'll fall with you—regardless of the Council's opinions or Procyon's status as a 'Protected Neutral' system."

"And I'm forever grateful to you for your help, old friend," Jenny says, still in what seems to be a better mood than she's been in for the last few months. "If it weren't for you and your 'household,' I'd just be leading a bunch of well-armed ducks sitting on the outskirts of each of our systems, waiting for the Novans to come conquering and hoping our allies could hold them off for us. I'm not all that keen on growing feathers anytime soon, you know?"

"You'd make a better heron than a duck, if my understanding of Earth's waterfowl is correct," Toreval remarks. "But I know what you mean." They pull their coat a little closer and try to ignore another shiver, growing quiet and lost in thoughts of home and the way things have turned out.

Jenny is right, of course; the so-called 'Quantum Space Drive' their people have shared with humanity puts the Defense Fleet on relatively equal footing with the ancient galactic powers whose long-running war they're all caught in. Without their corps of Florivan volunteers, the Fleet's ships would still be restricted to traveling at fractions of the speed of light. With their help, the same vessels can skip like stones between normal physical space and the veiled dimension of the Strange—crossing distances that would otherwise take decades in a matter of months.

Civilian vessels have been able to do that for decades, but Toreval argued long and hard with the rest of the Florivan Council of Elders to be permitted to leave their people's sanctuary at Procyon and become the first of their instinctively pacifist species to ever serve as a Quantum Space Drive Engineer on a military vessel. No matter what, Toreval still considers it a triumph on their part that the Council allows those who want to volunteer to help the Fleet to do so unhindered. Even as things stand now, six years later, their species is still officially neutral. Volunteers like Toreval choose a life of technical exile in order to join the Fleet and help protect their families and friends.

A memory flits across Toreval's mind of a conversation they had with two of their three eldest offspring and their human Ranger counterparts in the safety of their home on Procyon, not long after the news of the War first arrived. Then, Toreval was the one listening to an impassioned explanation of the danger the Novan Armada truly posed to everyone and everything in its way. Now, *they're* the one walking the path Iralee and Inayan had seen.

What would their kittens have thought, Toreval wonders, if they'd lived to see more than a hundred of their people volunteering to give up their personal status as members of a 'protected neutral species' in order to don the Fleet's colors? How would those two have reacted if they'd been there the day Toreval left Procyon with their Navigator, or if they could have seen everything that's happened since? Iralee and Inayan's surviving littermate *certainly* didn't take it well.

Toreval often tells themself that Iralee and Inayan would be proud of everything that's been done to honor their memory—assuming that one day there's an end to this and it hasn't all been for nothing. They can't allow themself to lose hope, but on days like this they can't help feeling drained.

"Are you feeling okay?"

"What?" Toreval is caught off-guard by the question. "Oh, I'm fine. Why?"

"You've been uncharacteristically quiet all afternoon, aside from a few moments ago." Jenny sets a hand briefly on Toreval's shoulder. "What is it, then?"

"Oh, just lost in thought." Toreval forces a shiver to turn into a laugh. "I will say, I never expected that I'd end up in more long, dull official talks as your advisor than I ever did for the Council—much less sitting in a glorified freezer for a strategy conference."

Jenny nods sympathetically. "Well, it's not every week we're trying to coordinate our forces directly with the T'irsh-fel for such a critical operation... and all things considered, it's probably for the best that they're hosting the talks."

"Of course," Toreval admits, "and it does seem to be going well so far from a *diplomatic* standpoint—I'm just not much for their idea of a comfortable habitat, that's all."

The T'irsh-fel are one of the two members of the greater Galactic Alliance involved in the war: an ancient and powerful species who mastered post-light travel several thousand years before they ever encountered other spacefaring peoples. Around half the size of an adult human, the thick-scaled T'irsh-fel evolved on a distant series of ice-covered moons. Unfortunately for Toreval, their idea of comfortable temperatures reflects that.

Even though one of the T'irsh-fel High Commander's attendants noticed Toreval shivering earlier and brought them an extra cloak to wear during the proceedings, they've still found themself chilled to the bone and wishing they'd worn more layers. The cold has been giving them twinges of pain in all their old scars, too—even the inner ones they stopped feeling regularly years ago. Toreval has mostly been able to ignore the aches so far, but it's hardly a pleasant way to go about one's day.

"Diplomacy does drag on a bit in the cold, doesn't it?" Jenny pulls off her coat altogether and drapes it over her arm before tapping the command pad on the lift that will take the two of them up to C deck and their respective quarters for some well-deserved rest.

"It does at that," Toreval agrees, making no move to shed any of their own layers of clothing. "Still, considering that the T'irsh-fel are *telepathic*? One would think that their High Commander wouldn't be the sort to argue the same points six times over even when he's *agreeing* with you."

"One would think, yes—but at least he's agreeing with me sooner or later."

Toreval shakes their head lightly. "Sometimes, Jenny, I wonder if it isn't just a universal truth among sapient species that where there's an organized society, there will be *meetings*... and ones that drag on at least twice as long as they should, at that."

"Oh, aside from the odd dictatorship? I wouldn't doubt it." Jenny chuckles. "Even with the Europans, it still takes ages sometimes for their queens to come to a consensus about important things—I mean, it took them *years* to decide they wanted the Alliance to register them as an 'Officially Non-Combatant Neutral/Protected Species,' even though we gave them all the information we had about that right when we were brought into the War. And they're even *more* of a eusocial species than y'all are."

"The Europans do have their own definition of 'urgent,' don't they?" Toreval remarks. The other sentient species native to the Sol system has the same status their own people do—aside from the Fleet's volunteers—but because they're a non-technological society with no real interests beyond their own small origin moon, rather than because they have an incredibly limited population and a pacifist tradition to uphold. Both peoples have been assured that this status will be respected by all of the Galactic Powers, whether involved in the war or not. Given the circumstances which led Toreval to take up the Admiral's cause in the first place, they *personally* don't trust the Novans to hold to that at all.

"They do at that," Jenny agrees. "Don't tell Glimmer, but I'd dare say that dealing with *your* Council is simple in comparison."

"You mean asking me to deal with them for you?" Toreval fixes her with a small wry smile of their own.

Jenny laughs brightly. "Wouldn't have it any other way, Celadon."

As they exit the lift a few moments later, Toreval sighs lightly.

"Something else on your mind?"

"Oh... I just can't help wishing the T'irsh-fel had reconsidered about letting me bring Li along. I know he's not much of a diplomat, but it'd certainly save us having to brief him on all of the strategy before the convoy leaves anyway."

Toreval doesn't say it out loud, but they also spent most of the day wishing their young human counterpart was there so they'd have someone sitting beside them who it wouldn't be "diplomatically undignified" to lean against for warmth. That's one of the best parts of having made their compact with a Navigator: humans may be a bit odd-looking, but they're *warm*. Jenny's a good enough friend that they know she wouldn't mind personally, but her position and the situation make it too awkward of a thing to ask. The woman from the Coalition Diplomatic Department who accompanied them today is barely an acquaintance, and one who wears strong perfume at that; in short, not someone worth sitting next to in the first place.

"True—I wouldn't be surprised if that little fiasco with Captain Zyzyk back when we were demonstrating the Drive tactics for them had more to do with the decision than their usual fixation on ranks..." Jenny shakes her head. "But in any case, it's good to have him getting all of my Captains and their Navigators ready for the operation in the meantime. I don't think there's anyone else I'd trust aside from Lieutenant Hsu to coordinate all of the jump drills and simulations while maintaining radio silence—or if there's anyone else who *could*, for that matter." Jenny smiles. She's had a maternal sort of fondness for Toreval's

Navigator ever since he was nothing more than a fresh-from-the-Academy Ensign serving as her assistant.

"I know." Toreval smiles lightly as well. "Li probably has the harder task this week, to be fair." Theirs is the best Navigator in the Fleet, after all—and Toreval's not the only one who thinks that. There's a reason he has a reputation as the Admiral's secret weapon among those who've seen his talents.

Toreval knows that what he's doing right now is important, but all the same, they've hardly even *seen* their Navigator today, between the long hours of meetings and shuttle flights and the sudden differences in their schedules. Even without the cold, that arrangement would make them uncomfortable. They'd never expected when they first met the young human just how strong their imprint on him would grow. Now, they're not sure how they ever managed without Li in their life.

Toreval is sure that once the Fleet's convoy finally sets off to face the Novan armada at its suspected base in the GJ-1061 system, they'll miss these boring but safe days and all the frigid bureaucracy that goes with them. At the moment, though, they really just want to curl up beside their Navigator under a blanket or two with a cup of tea and forget that they have the rest of a week of shuttle flights back and forth to the T'irsh-fel ship ahead of them—assuming all goes well and this strategy and diplomacy nonsense doesn't take *longer* to get sorted.

"Of course, Celadon," Jenny says, stopping at the door to her quarters for a moment before going in. "Feel free to tell him everything that goes on in these talks—the T'irsh-fel may not recognize him as one of my senior officers, but that's their problem. I'd like to have Lieutenant Hsu's opinion on things. You and I both know it's his skill we'll be relying on to pull off half of the things they're hoping we can do once we get there."

"I'll be sure to tell him you said that."

"See that you do."

Having bid their friend goodnight, Toreval walks the rest of the way down to their quarters with the pleasant thought that the only other person they'll have to interact with for the rest of the night is their Navigator. They're still chilled, sore, and tired enough that they don't like the idea of having to deal with other people at all.

Toreval walks into their quarters with that thought, only to be met with the unexpected sight of a visitor waiting patiently on their couch.

This visitor is a young human man wearing a non-commissioned officer's ivory uniform vest. The sleeves of the dark green shirt underneath are rolled up, and several of the topmost buttons unbuttoned. He's the ruddy-pale sort of human, with light brown hair that falls just to his shoulders. For once, though, he's tied that up halfway.

Toreval's first thought upon seeing him is the simple amused recognition that he seems to have finally taken their advice about how to keep his hair out of his face. This human, Elias Rudolph, is a dear friend—family, almost—and probably the only person in the galaxy aside from their Navigator or one of their kittens that they'd genuinely be pleased to see tonight. His presence may be unannounced, but they gave the man the codes to let himself in specifically *because* he's welcome in their quarters whenever he happens to be on their ship.

Toreval gives him a little wave while they're shedding their heavy insulated coat. The garment may have kept them a bit warm when they first set out this morning, but it's also *damp* from the frost in the cold, humid air of the T'irsh-fel ship. Thankfully, they have more comfortable clothes than a dress uniform soaked with a day's worth of accumulated ice water to change into.

After taking a few minutes in their bed-chamber to dry off and change into their favorite soft, thick-woven amber tunic and trousers, Toreval comes back out into the little sitting area in the middle of the quarters they share with their Navigator. One steaming cup of green tea acquired from the beverage dispenser in one of the wall panels, and they make themself comfortable on the other end of the couch from the visiting human.

Elias wordlessly pulls out the soft amber, yellow, and white striped blanket from the back of the couch behind him before Toreval can even ask and passes it to them.

Toreval nods their thanks and tucks the blanket over everything from their lower pair of arms down. They take particular care pulling their feet and long tufted tail up underneath the rest of their body so those can stand a chance of thawing out. The blanket might not be able to generate warmth for them, but at least it can keep what little body heat they still have from escaping.

"Li's still out running drills with the other Navigators," Toreval tells their visitor, finally able to relax a bit. "I think he should be coming back from *Strix* in an hour or so."

"Ah. I was about to ask—it's not usual I find one of you without the other nearby." The young human's voice is a *warm*, pleasant sort of sound with deep undertones that have always reminded Toreval a bit of the smell of coffee—but with none of the poisonous qualities of the beverage.

"It's an odd week." Toreval takes a sip from their tea. "So, Elias, what excuse do you have for stowing aboard to visit us this time?"

"Oh, hardly stowing aboard, Dons!" Elias laughs. "The maintenance team here needed some extra hands with their latest round of overhauls, so since everything's down for the radio-silence order anyway... I volunteered myself to help in exchange for a favor or two."

"And you're just a helpful person all around, aren't you?" Toreval chuckles. It's always refreshing to have him visit, even on a day like this when they're cold and damp and exhausted.

"Naturally. I even brought the day's pack of notes over from *Surnia* on my way. Glimmer has a long one for you in there, too. It's in your coms by now, but he made a point of asking me to tell you to look for it."

"Once my fingers thaw out enough that I can do that, I'll be sure to." Toreval takes another sip from their tea, savoring the warmth of it as they swallow. "How's Theodore doing, then?"

"Better, from what I've seen. I'd wager status updates on him are most of what Glimmer wants to tell you about." Elias shrugs. "It's good to see the kid up and moving more, even if he's still wobbly and a bit skittish when Indigo isn't around—not that I blame him for that."

"I'm sure." Toreval nods lightly. Their young friend Theodore is Jenny's current personal assistant, but for medical reasons, he and the Europan ambassador he's paired with have been on Elias' ship since the convoy left Kapteyn. They're glad to hear he's finally recovering from his injuries. "I'll have to send a note back for him tomorrow. Don't let me forget?"

"Will do."

After a pause to readjust the position of their legs, Toreval tilts their head curiously at Elias. "How long is this maintenance exchange running, then?"

"Three days, or until we get everything sorted. It's a nice change of pace—*Surnia's* run out of things for me to fix at the moment, believe it or not. With both squadrons either grounded to preserve radio silence or fighting over who gets to take carrier pigeon duty, it's the bad kind of quiet over there, anyway. Given the choice between being involved in the bloody prank war the Musketeers and the Lost Boys have going on or finding somewhere else to work..."

"You'd rather suffer through the shuttle flight to get here and deal with *our* bored and troublesome pilots instead?" Toreval gives him a bit of a knowing look with all three eyes over the top of their teacup. They know why Elias is really here, but playing along with his pretenses for visiting is part of the fun of being friends with him.

"Naturally." Elias gives them one of his signature cheeky grins. "And now that I'm here and finished with my tasks for the day and don't have anything else to do until second watch tomorrow, well... why not spend the time with my favorite jumper and see if they have any tech down in the Drive bay they could use some help tuning?"

"I just might take you up on that," Toreval says. Their friend isn't just a darter maintenance technician, after all.

Elias is a highly skilled communications engineer who's fully qualified to assist with the installation and upkeep of the specialized systems they and their Navigator use to keep *Aegolius'* crew safe during jumps through the Strange. "And I'd suspect you thought you'd surprise Li with a pleasant social call as well as long as you're in the neighborhood?"

"The thought *may* have occurred to me, yes." Elias feigns complete innocence, but there's a clear kitten-like eagerness in his voice. "Think he'd mind?"

"It'd probably be good for him, with the week we're about to have." Toreval takes another long sip from their tea and sets it on the table beside their end of the couch.

"Long one, then?"

"He's running sims and Nav training without me while I'm almost *literally* freezing my tail off with these strategy talks. It's just the first day and I'm already not sure who has it worse." Toreval sighs and starts trying to undo their still-soaked hair from its loops and the wooden ring and pin. All eight of the fingers on their upper pair of arms are being uncooperative. They haven't felt this sore and stiff in ages—not since the last time they lost an argument with the force of gravity, for sure.

"Do you want some help with that, Dons?" Elias chuckles lightly, gesturing towards their hair. "Looks like you could use a third pair of hands."

"Yes, please." Toreval sighs again and scoots over next to him, angling their body so he can reach their braids. "I don't know what the perfume is that this Coalition Diplomatic Protocol officer we're working with wears, but it's given me the worst headache..." They force back another shiver. "And my *everything* is still stiff from being in a series of freezers for the last twelve hours."

"No wonder you looked like you were frosted over when you came in."

"Elias," Toreval says dryly, "if this conference goes on much longer, Li's going to have a Florivan-shaped ice sculpture floating in the Drive Bay the next time he needs to call down landmarks."

Elias chuckles again. "Let's see if we can thaw you out before that happens, then."

Toreval relaxes and allows him to take down their braids and begin freeing their long silver hair from the ribbons so it can properly dry out in the relative warmth of their quarters. Aside from their Navigator and one of their old mentors, Elias is likely the only human they'd ever let touch them so casually. He's one of the only friends they have who they don't feel compelled to be some degree of formal around to begin with.

"Your ears are like ice," Elias comments, his hand brushing past one of them as he finishes un-braiding the first section of Toreval's hair. "Do they hurt?"

"Yes, but not more than anything *else* of mine does right now," Toreval admits. "I'm fine, but we're not really made for dealing with the cold. It's... uncomfortable, to say the least."

"I can see that." Elias gently rubs some warmth back into their ears. "Is this better?"

"...Yes, thank you." Toreval nods, instinctively leaning into his touch as they do.

Normally, Toreval would be somewhat embarrassed to allow themself to be petted like a kitten at all. They're an adult, and, more importantly, an *Elder*. Even with their own parent and siblings they'd be expected to maintain some level of decorum even in private because of that. At the moment, though, they're still chilled and this human is trustworthy and particularly warm, even for his species.

From almost the moment they met him, Elias has easily been their favorite person in the galaxy aside from their kittens and their Navigator. Toreval still hasn't figured out quite how or why that happened, but they're glad that it has. He's a good friend to have.

It doesn't hurt that their Navigator has become close with him, of course. They suspect Li's growing fondness for this particular human is part of why they've formed such a strong imprint on him themself. If Li has to be the sort of human who ultimately needs to have a companion from his own species to be happy, Toreval is glad that the current prospect for that position is someone they'd be pleased to have around even if Li *wasn't* interested in him.

It also doesn't hurt, particularly today, that Elias is always warm. It's soothing, being close to that kind of warmth for a change. Space is cold, after all, and humans keep their ships right on the edge of uncomfortably cool by Florivan standards most of the time. Not as bad as the T'irsh-fel ship, by any means, but if it weren't for the long sleeves and layers of their uniform, Toreval probably wouldn't be able to stand being in the colder parts of *Aegolius* for very long either. At least they can keep their quarters a few degrees warmer. Their Navigator is from one of the hotter climate regions of the Luyten's Star colony, and he's almost as cold-natured as a human can get because of that.

"Are you sure you're okay?" Elias asks after a few minutes,

returning to working those warm alien fingers of his through their remaining braids.

"Mm... no, I'm fine... just tired." Toreval stifles a yawn. They're very aware of the tiredness, now that they're being still and no one's expecting them to answer hard questions or pay attention to strategies.

It's easy to just let all three of their eyes slip closed, now that they're somewhere quiet and away from other people.

It's even easier to slip into the warm dreamless darkness of sleep.

★

A TYPICAL DAY'S EVENTS FOR PETTY OFFICER Third Class Elias Rudolph are relatively straightforward. He wakes up in time to start what passes for a night shift on SCV *Surnia*, acquires coffee, checks in with the ship's Nav/Quan team to see if they need help with any of their tech before they start the night's Quantum Space Transit cycle, retrieves his missing tools from a certain overly helpful Florivan kitten, and spends the rest of his time fixing anything his pilots have managed to break while he was off-duty.

The Second Darter Squadron may only be made up of one wing team of four pilots, but Elias swears he has just as much work keeping them flying as the whole three-person team responsible for maintaining the darters for a full four-wing squadron like *Surnia's* other unit, the 18th. Most of the maintenance technicians he knows from the Defense Fleet's other squadrons would agree with him, too. His pilots have a well-earned reputation for being both the Fleet's best fliers and its most notorious troublemakers.

Today, though, Elias is lucky enough to be taking a break from dealing with their antics. The Musketeers won't be flying until the convoy sets off on its mission, leaving the four of them bored but thankfully not causing more work for Elias in the meantime. *Yet.* A favor owed to one of his mechanic buddies was as good an opportunity as any to have a way to be on a different ship when the inevitable fallout from the pilots' usual ways of combating boredom comes down.

Even luckier for Elias, his buddy CPO Quince is the head maintenance technician for *Aegolius'* First Squadron. If there's any ship worth enduring a shuttle flight to get to for a few days, this is it. That's a considerable thing, in Elias' book: he's prone enough to spacesickness that he avoids getting on any of the smaller spacecraft as much as he possibly can. If it weren't for the mix of anti-nausea medication and mild sedative a doctor friend had sorted out for him when he first wound up assigned to *Surnia*, he wouldn't be able to stand shuttle flights over twenty minutes. Proper starships don't bother him most of the time, thankfully. Even so, Elias habitually wears mag-sole work boots even when he's not on duty in the darter bays just in case there's a shift in *Surnia's* internal artigrav systems. Even if no one else can distinguish the sensation when the fields aren't tuned correctly, *he* can—much to his discomfort—and the bouncing around that happens in microgravity is just as bad as flight.

He expected that discomfort this morning, though, and it was worth it to get to *Aegolius* for a few days. He even had a decent time helping poor Quince reassemble the stabilizer rigging on a darter straight after arrival. Working the day shift isn't his preference, but the work needed to be done and it's not like he *needs* to be on specific hours when the convoy's just sitting around like it is.

Somehow, though, Elias never expected that he'd end up spending the better part of two or three hours after his duty shift lounging on a couch reading technical update journals with *Aegolius*' QSD Engineer sleeping snuggled up against him like some odd alien cat. Then again, he'd never expected to become friends with this particular Florivan at all, nor that a single chance encounter with them would change the course of his life forever.

Elias has been friends with Celadon Toreval for just over a year now, but he's never seen them like this before. There's something downright *vulnerable* about a person who's fallen asleep and snuggled up to whoever was closest to them at the time. Vulnerability isn't something he ever thought to associate with them at all. Dons, as he's settled on calling them, is usually the most composed person in the galaxy.

Elias continues lightly stroking behind Dons' soft catlike ears the same way he's been doing since they first fell asleep. He's moved all of their now-dry hair out of the way so nothing can accidentally catch on it, but their ears were still cold when he finished taking out their braids, so it just seemed the thing to do. All four of his friend's arms, meanwhile, are either tucked up close to their body or loosely clinging on to him. Somewhere underneath the second blanket he pulled down from the back of the couch, their long tufted tail has wrapped itself around the lower part of one of his legs. Most of their face is nestled into the fabric of his uniform vest, obscuring the fine silver tiger stripes that mark the majority of their pale greenish-blue skin. A pleasant, soft rumbling sound is emanating from them, too: less of a snore and more of a cat's purr overlaid with the deep, oscillating tone of a ringing crystal goblet.

The whole experience reminds him of home, particularly of the blind grey and white cat his grandmother kept on her homestead on Teegarden b. Old Tom was the sort of cat whose trust had to be earned—Elias still bears more than one scar on his hands from the process—but once that cat *did* decide you were his, it was best to just accept the honor and let Old Tom sleep on your lap as long as he wanted.

Elias knows Dons is supposed to be an "Elder" or something like that, so perhaps the comparison isn't all that far off—although they've never seemed all that old to him. He's never thought about it at the right time to ask how old they really are. He does know that they have one kid his age, though, and one that's still a teenager, so "old enough to theoretically be his parent" is his best guess. All the same, Elias is relatively sure they're not even middle-aged yet as far as Florivans go.

In any case, his friendship with Dons has nothing to do with age or titles. The two of them have simply gotten along on an almost instinctive level from their first meeting. It's an easy, comfortable sort of a friendship, too. Whenever people bring up how odd of a combination a high-ranking

Florivan officer and a scruffy young mechanic should be, Elias normally falls back on an answer along the lines of "we both like coconut cocktails without the booze and think their Navigator is bloody *wonderful*," usually with a bit of sarcasm thrown in for good measure. Both statements are true, though—as is the fact that Dons is the best card-playing partner Elias has ever found. His pilots have yet to defeat the pair of them at Snapdragon's Garden.

Minor points of commonality aside, though, if Elias is honest with himself it's more that Dons is the sibling he never had as a child and always wanted. It's odd, considering the apparent age gap and the fact that the two of them are from entirely different species, but it's true. As near as he can tell, he seems to have filled a similar emptiness in their life too. He doesn't get to spend enough time around Dons, though, to have had a chance to ask if he's right about that.

Any musings he might have been making on the subject disappear from his mind at the sound of the cabin door beeping and sliding open.

The attractive, tawny-pale man with the long black ponytail who enters is, after all, Elias' main reason for finding excuses to come over from *Surnia* whenever he can. He's certainly reason enough to have all other thoughts disappear, too. Li is good at making entrances, even though he doesn't try to be. The long green and ivory scarf he wears with his crisply pressed officer's uniform certainly doesn't hurt the dashing image of the man.

"I have to say, this isn't what I expected I'd be coming home to at all."

"Jealous, Lieutenant?" Elias quips, keeping his voice slightly lowered.

Li laughs brightly, shaking his head. "A little, maybe, but I've got no idea which one of you I'm supposed to be jealous *of*."

Elias chuckles too, although quietly. "To be fair," he says, still keeping his voice barely above a whisper, "I was just helping Dons with their hair so it could dry while we were waiting for you... and then they sort of melted and fell asleep on me."

"Then it's pretty much what it looks like." Li comes over to the couch and sits perched on the armrest beside Elias' shoulder, looking down at the serene face of his sleeping counterpart with a soft smile.

"I have to say, Li, I *really* wasn't expecting the purring. I'd have thought that was something they grew out of." Elias is entirely too familiar with the silver fluff of a Florivan kitten one of his pilots is raising and their much smaller version of the purr. Somehow he'd never considered that adult Florivans would have the same reaction to having their ears petted. It's a much nicer sound when it's not coming from someone who constantly tries to borrow his tools while he's working, though.

"Val doesn't do it often. It means they trust you, if they're that relaxed."

"I'm honored, then." Elias looks up to meet his favorite pair of dark brown eyes in the galaxy and smiles. "I almost hate to wake them."

"You don't have to just yet. It's actually kind of cute seeing the two of you like this."

"You *would* think that, wouldn't you?"

"I *may* be a bit biased."

"I'm sure you are, Li."

Li snorts softly and reaches out a hand to ruffle the closer side of Elias' hair and make it all fall free from the thin hairband that had been holding it back out of his face.

This is the side of him that Elias likes best. Just like his counterpart, Li keeps a lot to himself when he's out in public. He's the sort of man who's very formal about his work and his role in the Fleet. It's part of his charm that things like protocols and personnel regulations actually *matter* to him, even—but having been the Admiral's protégé must have that effect on a person. Still, being around him when he's relaxed and casually affectionate like this is a thing to be treasured, in Elias' mind.

"I'm just glad to see them sleeping at all, you know?" Li says, looking down at Dons again after a moment.

"Oh?"

"They think I don't notice, but I know they've barely slept lately—even if Florivans don't need as many hours as we do, it's just not normal for Val to go so long without resting." It's obvious from Li's tone of voice that he's worried. Elias has heard Dons use the same tone more than once, too, when Li's neglected to take care of himself and they've wanted help sorting it out. It stands to reason, though; Li and Dons have been taking care of each other for years, after all. It would be odd if they didn't worry over each other at least a bit.

"Think it's because of stress?"

"Yeah…" Li pauses, making a little shrug. "That, and they had a long call over the relays with the Council the day before we went radio-silent and there was a pointed lack of conversation about it afterwards, which means that either it was some internal Florivan thing they're not ready to tell me about yet... or the fact that Jade still won't talk to them is weighing on them again."

"Jade's their kid that's stayed on Procyon, right?"

"The one I've never properly met who hates my guts even more than Val's parent does for 'enticing them away from the safety of the Sanctuary,' yeah." Li makes a vague air quotation gesture and then sighs lightly. "Well, as much as Florivans are actually *capable* of hating folks, at least."

"Ah. Right. So family drama, then." Elias is familiar with family drama. His own clan has too much of it, in his opinion. There's enough between his mother and her sisters that it was one of his secondary reasons for enlisting in the Fleet as soon as he came of age. He isn't completely clear on all of the details of Dons' situation, but what little he knows about their estrangement from their family— and how important those family bonds are for a member of a semi-eusocial species like theirs—makes Elias want to visit Procyon himself and tie a knot in the tail of anyone who's set on ostracizing them.

"Yeah... if there's anything else going on, they haven't mentioned it to me."

Elias gives Li's arm a reassuring pat with his free hand. "Well, I don't know about the rest," he says, "but it might just be because they've been stuck in the Admiral's meetings with the T'irsh-fel. They were all chilled and grumbling about that when they got in, at least."

"Heh. Simple as that?" Li stifles a laugh. "You're right. That's probably why they're so happy snuggling with *you* right now, too, now that I think about it."

"What, just because I'm warm?" He wouldn't be surprised if that was the case. The same set of inherited gene mods responsible for his issues with space-sickness are the ones that make his natural body temperature run higher than an average human's.

"Well, you have to admit, Elias, you *are* cozy."

"Either that or *you're* just every bit as cold-natured as Dons is," Elias teases. "I mean, you two keep this place what, ten degrees above the rest of the ship?"

"Only five, actually. Either way, it's good to see them actually relax for once."

"Glad I could help, then."

After a moment, Li leans over closer to his ear. "So, Elias... not that I'm unhappy to see you or anything, but what in the *stars* are you doing here?"

"Oh, you know... Came over to help the maintenance folks here for the next day or two, thought I'd offer to take you out to dinner—well, as 'out' as one can get on a ship, at least—which I'm still offering, assuming that I can find a polite way to get up."

"You're sweet."

"I do try."

Li rewards the sweetness with a quick peck on his cheek. "I think Val would be okay with being woken up—although I wouldn't put it past them to fall asleep on you again sometime if you let them."

"I wouldn't mind if they did, to be fair," Elias admits. "This is kind of nice."

Li reaches over and moves Elias' hand off of the sleeping Florivan's head, then sets his own in its place. "Come on, Val," he says, tickling Dons lightly behind one of their ears. "I know Elias is warm and comfortable, but you need to wake up so we can go get *food*."

After a minute or two, Dons yawns and makes a series of reluctant sleepy kitten sounds before finally opening their three golden eyes and looking up at the two humans. It's amusing, somehow, that this is the same person that everyone outside this room knows as the Admiral's most trusted advisor and a wise, serious sort of alien Elder figure. In the moment, Elias can't help but think they're just as adorable as the much smaller Florivan who *usually* falls asleep on him.

"*Mrrr*? Oh, hello, Li. I didn't hear you come in..."

"I just got back from *Strix* a few minutes ago. Have a nice nap?"

Dons stifles another yawn. "...I don't remember falling asleep."

Elias grins down at them. "Fell asleep and then some—at least you didn't try to crawl into my pockets like Wyndi does."

"Oh." Dons seems incredibly embarrassed, for some reason. "I'm sorry—"

"No worries, Dons, anytime. What else are friends for?" Elias carefully extracts himself from their collection of limbs and stands, stretching out his legs. "So, are you two fine upstanding officers in a mood for being taken to dinner by a lowly maintenance tech or not?"

Dons also stretches, but doesn't get up off of the couch. Elias wouldn't be surprised if they're hesitant to leave the residual warmth under the blanket, considering how much they were shivering earlier. "Oh, you two go on and enjoy yourselves. I'm not up to being around people any more today... but I'll take a rain check for sometime before you go back to *Surnia*."

"Rain check is yours, Dons. Piña coladas are on me whenever you feel like you can handle the ice, too."

"I'd like that... maybe not with *any* ice until this conference is over, though."

"Fair."

Li gives his counterpart an affectionate pat on the shoulder and stands up from his perch on the armrest. "I'll see you later, then, Val. Want me to bring you back something from the mess?"

"...No, thank you." Dons is already curling back up under the blanket. "Not particularly hungry at the moment... Too cold. Maybe later?"

"All right, then. Ping me if you change your mind."

As Elias and Li are leaving, Dons calls out to them teasingly from underneath the blanket. "Just try not to get into any trouble tonight, will you? It's no fun having to talk Jenny out of throwing you in the brig if I don't get to be there to start the trouble in the first place."

Both men get a good laugh out of that on their way to the crew mess. As far as Elias is concerned, the shuttle flight this morning was well worth suffering through for the chance to be with his favorite pair of officers for a few days.

A**NOTHER DAY INTO THE STRATEGY DISCUSSIONS** on the T'irsh-fel ship, and Toreval is sitting under a heat lamp one of the High Commander's assistants has procured for them in the private chamber off of the main conference room and trying to thaw out enough that they'll be able to concentrate for the rest of the day. It's quite kind of this particular attendant to have even thought to set such a thing up at all, and to have once again brought them a particularly thick cloak to wrap over their layers of uniform and coat.

The heat lamp and the cloak, though, are barely enough warmth to cut through the damp chill of Toreval's own uniform and allow them to do something other than sit and try not to visibly shiver. It's a nice gesture, if anything. Still, all they can think of is how nice it will be to be done with the day's discussion of maneuvers and responsibilities and tucked into their nice warm nest on Aegolius—preferably with one or both of their nice warm humans tucked in with them.

*Are you well, Commander Celadon, Sir?*

A young T'irsh-fel girl waves several eye-stalks in Toreval's direction as she slithers in through the chamber's doorway curtain. Telepathy or not, the "sound" of Attendant Ryzyk's words in the back of their mind is clearly colored with concern. She's been hovering around them all day, although Toreval can't imagine why. Small for her species but sporting a lovely ruff of red feathers around the area where her eight long mobile eye-stalks connect to the rest of her thick-scaled, limbless body, Ryzyk seems to have taken it upon herself to be Toreval's minder. Whether she's been ordered to do that or not is anyone's guess.

"Oh, don't worry about me, Attendant Ryzyk," they reply. "Are the others ready to start talking again?"

*The refreshment period is still ongoing.*

Ryzyk inclines one of her eye-stalks towards the door curtain behind her.

*This humble self wished to inquire if you were certain you do not desire to partake in the mid-cycle meal with the other guests.*

Toreval shakes their head lightly. "Ah, no, thank you—and please convey to your people that my absence is not meant as an offense. Your hospitality is greatly appreciated. It's simply that the cold has a way of slowing down our metabolisms considerably... and making even the thought of food thoroughly unappealing. I'm content to sit here where it's a touch warmer and gather my thoughts."

*As you wish, Commander Celadon, Sir...*

There's a hesitancy to the thought projection this time. Ryzyk swivels several of her eye stalks to look over Toreval more carefully.

"Is something bothering you, Attendant Ryzyk?" Toreval asks, tilting their head curiously. "I won't be offended by anything you have to say, truly. My people value being open with our concerns. As our Eldest would say: 'if it isn't spoken, how can we know what to do about it?'"

The young T'irsh-fel bobs all of her eye stalks briefly.

*This humble self apologizes that she has not been able to do more to see to your comfort. The concerns of the ship's honored Ranking Engineer that a higher temperature than this could lead to considerable damage to our systems even outside this room were insurmountable.*

"No need to apologize." Toreval absently withdraws their upper pair of hands from within the layers of their clothing and holds them up closer to the heat lamp in hopes of thawing their fingers out a bit. "You've been wonderfully accommodating, Attendant Ryzyk, and I'm certainly warmer now than I was yesterday, thanks to you."

*This humble self thanks you for the compliment—*

Young Ryzyk seems about to ask something else, but she's interrupted by Jenny's sudden appearance in the doorway.

"I brought you something vaguely resembling tea, Commander," she says, coming over to Toreval and holding out a translucent green cup full of steaming liquid. "And I've been assured that it is, in fact, safe for you to drink. I'd suggest you do that before it has time to freeze solid."

Toreval smiles softly, accepting the cup with both of their semi-thawed hands. It's the first genuine warmth they've felt since they got on the T'irsh-fel shuttlecraft this morning. "Thank you, Admiral. Should I consider that suggestion an order?"

"If you're still set on not eating lunch with me and Ms. Harrington and making small talk with our hosts? Yes." Jenny fixes them with that signature no-nonsense expression she has that reminds them so much of their parent.

"Yes, ma'am." Toreval takes a small sip from the cup. It's *sweet* more than having any particular flavor, but hot enough to actually warm their insides as they swallow. "Thank you."

"Attendant Ryzyk," Jenny says, looking to the young T'irsh-fel, "since I'm obligated to return to the refreshment room, would you be so kind as to stay with Commander Celadon and make sure they follow my orders?"

*Yes, Admiral Marvin, Sir. This humble self will be honored to follow your request.*

Ryzyk scoots herself over nearer to Toreval, just outside the reach of the lamp's warm glow.

"Thank you." With that, Jenny leaves them.

If it's anything like the first day of the talks, she likely won't be back for another hour. The T'irsh-fel High Commander seems to take his mealtimes quite seriously; he outright refuses to talk business over food. It's another cultural quirk that Toreval hasn't figured out yet, even having worked with this species off and on for several years now.

*Your most honored Admiral Marvin is remarkable, to*

*personally attend to one of her subordinates.*

Ryzyk's eyes turn back to Toreval now, with a note of awed curiosity in her mental tone.

*She shows you the highest of honors.*

"She is a dear friend as much as she is my Admiral," Toreval says, pausing to take another sip from the sweet steaming beverage they're holding. "But I'd agree that she's one of the more remarkable humans I've worked with."

They mean this, too. Jenny's proven herself time and again to be exactly the sort of person they'd always hoped their eventual Captain would be, back when they were a kitten dreaming of a life in the stars. She's able to lead not only her own ship, but the entire Defense Fleet with grace and wisdom. Her kindness and confidence balance each other nicely.

Six years on from meeting Jenny for themself, it's clear to Toreval now that their two dear kittens who the War has taken from them had been right about her. They can't imagine anyone else who they would have been willing to entrust with the lives and safety of their people, nor who they would rather serve with. Toreval's always thought she would have made a fine Elder, if she'd been Florivan instead of human—probably a better one than they are, at that.

Toreval's quiet consideration of the matter is interrupted by a gently projected thought.

*Are you certain you're well, Commander Celadon, Sir?*

Toreval looks over to the T'irsh-fel girl with an amused flick of their ears. "Oh, yes. I'm fine. Why do you ask?"

*You have been staring into your drink long enough now that it has ceased steaming.*

One of Ryzyk's eye stalks swivels to pointedly look at the cup in their hands.

*In fact, it is beginning to form ice crystals on the surface.*

"Oh?" Toreval looks down. The young T'irsh-fel is right. "I must have been lost in my thoughts..." They take a curious sip from the portion that's still liquid. It's still incredibly sweet and oddly floral, but *entirely* too cold to be worth drinking now. They set the cup down on the bench beside them. "Don't tell my Admiral I didn't finish all of it?" They stifle a chilled laugh.

*This humble self will acquire a refreshed beverage for you so that you may properly comply with your most honored Admiral's orders.*

Ryzyk focuses several of her eyes on the green cup sitting beside Toreval. After a few moments, it floats up and goes to hover in front of her. T'irsh-fel short-range telekinesis never ceases to impress.

*Perhaps in an insulated container with a lid, so that you may take it into the conference room with you?*

Toreval smiles and gives her a small nod. "Thank you, Attendant Ryzyk. That would be lovely."

After Ryzyk has scooted her way out the door with the green cup floating obediently behind her, Toreval pulls up their legs and tries to find a more heat-preserving position to sit in until their new friend comes back. They sincerely hope that they and Jenny will be able to work out all of the details for the convoy's operation by the end of the day. As nice as Ryzyk is, they can't wait to be back with Li and Elias on a ship that's at least *somewhat* warm.

✦

Hours later, Toreval is doing their best to follow the conversation that Jenny is having with Ms. Harrington, the visiting officer from the Sol Coalition Diplomatic Service. It isn't easy. The small T'irsh-fel shuttlecraft ferrying the three of them back to *Aegolius* is just as cold as the High Admiral's ship, and with how long the day has dragged on, Toreval's mind can't help but wander. They're grateful that the shuttle's plush floor cushions are large enough that they can fully pull their legs up underneath themself to conserve a bit more of their remaining warmth. The small bench-top cushions on the High Commander's ship and the need to maintain their "dignified Florivan Elder and advisor to the Admiral" persona have been conspiring together to keep Toreval from finding a reasonably comfortable position during the long, frigid hours of the strategy talks. Their tail is neatly tucked around their waist inside the uniform jacket they're wearing under their thicker coat, but it's still taken on enough of a chill that they can barely feel it.

"Ma'am, I assure you," Ms. Harrington says, deftly swishing her overly-perfumed black shawl back over her shoulder, "following the correct protocols for interaction with our allies can only lead to a mutually beneficial result."

Toreval still isn't sure what to think of the short blonde woman who came aboard their ship before the convoy left Kapteyn. She's more of a stickler for protocol than any human they've ever met, for sure. That isn't bad in itself, but coupled with her somewhat grating attitude towards the competence and intelligence of those around her and her apparent sense of superiority as a civilian advisor *assigned* to Jenny by the Sol Coalition's greater leadership, she is proving somewhat difficult for the rest of *Aegolius'* staff to get along with. Even their own usually even-tempered and charming Navigator has clashed with her—most recently over her insistence that the T'irsh-fel Admiralty was correct to bar him from attending these talks.

Toreval themself would probably feel more charitable towards her today if the sharp musky smell of her perfume wasn't soaking into them and making their head hurt even more than the long damp hours in the cold already has. They don't understand why she feels the need to cover up her natural scent with something *stronger* any more than they do why she keeps re-folding her shawl and inadvertently wafting it in their direction.

"I understand what you're saying, Ms. Harrington," Jenny replies. She loosely crosses her arms over her chest. "But I'd appreciate if you refrained from correcting me in front of the T'irsh-fel again. I've been working with them long enough now to know that being *undermined* by my subordinates publicly only weakens my position in their eyes."

"Bear in mind, Admiral Marvin," Ms. Harrington says dryly, "that I am *not* one of your subordinates. I am here to advise you and preempt any diplomatic incidents."

"And *I* am here to lead the Fleet on an operation of unprecedented scale with our allies." Jenny does not show any signs of backing down, nor of losing her temper. From what Toreval understands, she's had variations on this conversation with Ms. Harrington ever since the woman showed up unannounced with her orders from the Coalition Diplomatic Service the day they left Kapteyn.

Granted, if *Aegolius'* resident Europan Ambassador wasn't tied up with his own human counterpart's ongoing recovery from a near-death experience at the hands of a Novan spy, there wouldn't have been a reason for the Coalition Diplomatic Corps to send someone along in the first place. Glimmer is, after all, a fully qualified Coalition diplomat in his own right, and his translator is Jenny's personal assistant. The T'irsh-fel like both of them, too. It would have been far simpler sorting out these strategy talks if those two were able to attend instead of Ms. Harrington.

The amusing thought of what will happen if Ms. Harrington ever crosses paths with Elias flits through Toreval's mind. Li, at least, keeps his opinions of people to himself in public. Only someone who knows him as well as Toreval and Jenny do can tell when he genuinely dislikes someone based on how he carries himself around them. Elias, though, isn't as skilled at concealing his opinions or his temper. He also has little patience for hubris or self-important people in positions of authority.

On second consideration, Toreval decides it might be best to do what they can to make sure their friend and Ms. Harrington never encounter each other. They'd rather not see Elias get in trouble with her civilian government connections right when Jenny herself is finally starting to show signs of warming up to him.

"Of course you are, Admiral." It's hard to tell if the condescending note on the edge of Ms. Harrington's tone is intentional, or if she's entirely unaware of it. "Still, it never hurts to be polite to our allies—"

*Commander Celadon, sir?*

The T'irsh-fel pilot's mental voice distracts Toreval again

from the conversation.

*This humble self would like to ask if you wish to sit with him for the remainder of the flight. It would be an honor to consider the stars with you.*

When Toreval glances up, they see that he's extended a single eye stalk through the shimmering curtain separating his control compartment from the passenger area to look in their direction. His people's telepathy is based in their line of sight, from what Toreval understands. Just as with most of the doorways on their ship, the easily-moved curtain is the T'irsh-fel answer to the need for both passenger privacy and easy communication from the pilot.

Toreval nods and stands, albeit with a certain annoying stiffness to their limbs. They're not certain why he's made the offer, but it's better than sitting and listening to Ms. Harrington pester Jenny. Perhaps moving around a bit will help them thaw out, too.

"—And I don't think—wait. Celadon?" Jenny asks, doing little to mask the note of concern in her voice.

"Our pilot is curious about Florivan star-marking," they reply, making their way forward to the curtain. "Don't worry, I'll be able to hear you if anything you discuss calls for my opinion." They make an absent gesture at their somewhat numb ears.

Jenny nods and goes back to her conversation.

Toreval slips through the curtain. They do appreciate how nice a view the T'irsh-fel pilot has of the star-scape around the halted convoy's ships. A grand swath of the galaxy stretches across the hemispherical bubble which serves as both viewport and enclosing structure for the pilot's area. So too can they see both the small starship they now call home and the far larger T'irsh-fel cruiser they've been on all day. As with most QSD-equipped starships, *Aegolius* has inherited its design from a mix of Florivan and human sensibilities; the result is resemblant of a large grey-striped fish with solar sails for fins, if one has the imagination to see it. Meanwhile, the T'irsh-fel cruiser is shimmering and angular, like a great bismuth crystal dotted with hemispherical bubbles and sporting three blue-lit main engine structures on one end. Toreval has no idea how the T'irsh-fel post-light engines work, of course, but the design of their housings lends a nice aesthetic.

"Thank you," they say softly, looking down to the pilot. He's seated on a wide golden cushion with a vast array of dials and button controls surrounding the set of readout screens in front of him. "The view is lovely."

The pilot shifts the lower portion of his body to one side, turning three of his eye-stalks to Toreval now.

*You are welcome to sit, Commander Celadon, Sir. This humble self begs forgiveness for his accidental eavesdropping, but it seemed that you might appreciate an excuse to be somewhere quieter.*

"It's much appreciated." Toreval stifles a chuckle as they take a seat beside the pilot on his cushion. They're surprised to find that the pilot's body heat has left it rather warm. There's a lot that they don't know about his species, of course, but they genuinely hadn't considered that the T'irsh-fel's biology included *shedding* heat.

*Please be assured that this humble self will keep any conversations he overhears among your companions private. In normal circumstances, he would simply keep the curtain closed...*

While the pilot speaks to them, the majority of his focus is clearly still on flying. Every now and again, the little dials, buttons, and switches on his control console move seemingly on their own as testament to his attention to his task.

"...But that doesn't work with species who converse out loud instead of directing their thoughts to the specific people they want to hear them." Toreval nods. "I'll have to mention that to the two of them later."

*That would be most appreciated, Commander Celadon, Sir.*

The pilot fluffs the deep orange feathers of his neck ruff appreciatively for a moment.

*It would be grievously impolite to allow one's passengers to converse candidly within one's hearing without warning them that their words might be remembered... and asked after.*

"I see what you mean, Pilot..." Toreval looks at him curiously. "Forgive me, I don't recall if I was told your name."

*This humble self is formally called Zyrr.*

"Pilot Zyrr, then." Toreval nods.

After a few moments of silence, aside from the soft clicking of Zyrr's flight controls and the not-at-all-hard to overhear conversation on the other side of the curtain in the background, he turns his attention back to Toreval.

*May this humble self make a small candid comment to you, Commander Celadon, Sir, regarding matters which he might have overheard?*

"Of course." Toreval is still cold and their mind still wants to wander, but being able to soak up a touch of the residual warmth on the pilot's large floor cushion and watch the comforting lights of the galaxy is centering. Not to mention their undeniable curiosity about what his comments might be.

*Your Admiral is correct. It is anathema to us to talk over or publicly undermine a person in direct authority. Etiquette demands discretion when critiquing leadership—comments will be heard, perhaps listened to if correct, but one must be polite.*

Zyrr makes a particular swish of one of his eye stalks for emphasis.

*To breach etiquette too severely can be one's downfall.*

"My Admiral has worked with your people since they first contacted humanity. She's quite familiar with the realities of your etiquette as it applies to us." Toreval can't feel their ears well enough to know if they've made an appropriate twitching motion towards the curtain. "We've been assured that Ms. Harrington is a skilled diplomat," they add softly enough that only someone right next to them could hear, "but humans have different ideas sometimes about what respect of authority looks like, or how it should be performed in front of others."

*And among your people?*

Toreval has to think through their response. "We're taught to be polite and respect that our Elders make decisions for the benefit of all of us, and that those who are older than us have wisdom and experience which should be listened to. An Elder is respected, yes, and the authority of their household... but we make a point of considering all of the opinions and needs of our kittens when making our decisions. I *represent* my household to the Council, if that makes any sense?"

*Some. This humble self will further consult the cultural archives on your society's structure later, so that he may converse with you tomorrow with a greater baseline knowledge—if you would be interested in discussing the ways of our respective peoples further, that is.*

He lightly ruffles his feathers again.

*It is a rare delight for a humble Pilot to converse with his passengers on matters other than flying.*

Toreval smiles. "I'd like that, Pilot Zyrr. It would certainly keep me awake long enough to get through these shuttle flights."

*If you wish to rest instead, Commander Celadon, Sir, this humble self will not be offended...*

"Ah, no, that's not what I mean." Toreval almost feels their ears twitch this time. "The lower temperatures make it hard for me to focus and stay alert after a long day of meetings, that's all. I mean to say I'd welcome a bit of conversation if I won't prove too much of a distraction for you."

*This humble self considers you a truly delightful distraction, Commander Celadon, Sir.*

The light bobbing of the three eye-stalks he has focused on them remind Toreval, somehow, of a human waggling their eyebrows cheekily.

*Although, he will not deny that it concerns him that you are being so affected by our preferred climate.*

"I'll be fine," Toreval assures him. "Once I'm back on *Aegolius,* I'll be able to properly thaw out. I'll be ready to finish these meetings off tomorrow, you'll see." They manage to put enough cheerful confidence in their voice that they almost believe themself, too. "I doubt it will take more than that for my Admiral and your High Commander to sort everything out."

*If you say so, Commander Celadon, Sir, Zyrr replies.*

There's a confusing trace of hesitation in the mental projection of his voice.

*If you say so...*

★

Six days after he first left *Surnia* for his temporary personnel exchange assignment, Elias is busy in *Aegolius'* main shuttle bay. The task of the day is relatively simple, in his mind. It's little more than helping sort out an issue with the communications relay system on one of the older shuttles. Even though it won't be needed until the convoy is out of radio silence orders, the more small tasks like this that can be handled while they're all sitting around waiting for the Admiral to finish her strategy negotiations with the T'irsh-fel, the fewer things will be lying in wait to go wrong once they get underway.

Elias has always liked working with relay tech. It's a crucial system, even for small craft like this shuttle that use it for little more than keeping in contact with a mother ship.

The whole greater Relay Network the shuttle's systems are designed to tap into is what allows the Defense Fleet and the inhabitants of humanity's systems to keep in contact and have access to information in near real time over the vast distances of space.

Like the Quantum Space Drive, the Relay Network has its origins in the close friendship between humanity and the Florivans. Unlike the Drive, though, the relay tech was easily sorted out and adapted so that any human engineer with a high enough skill rating can be reasonably expected to keep it working. The tiny quantum entanglement crystals in the receivers were first developed for use with the com links a Navigator uses to keep in contact with their counterpart while the Drive is active and the ship is in the middle of Quantum Space, but the tech obeys the laws of physics closely enough to allow them to be used elsewhere.

While Elias currently serves in the Fleet as a darter maintenance technician, he got his start working on relay, Nav/Quan, and communications tech development at the Shell Island base at Teegarden's Star. That's why *Surnia*'s Captain Brentwood and her Nav/Quan team were keen on helping the Musketeers claim him for their squadron's mechanic: they got a spare relay and nav tech man out of the deal. For Elias, those sorts of systems are intuitive. Child's play, even, for the sort of simple relay crystal arrays that darters and small shuttles carry.

Those simple crystal arrays also, *apparently*, are just as easy for shuttle pilots to break as they are for the Musketeers.

And so it is that Elias has spent most of the afternoon wedged underneath the belly of a rather old shuttle, rerouting circuits to finish up a temporary workaround so things will be marginally functional while he's making the *actual* repairs elsewhere. A pair of uniformed legs and smartly polished boots are standing just within his peripheral vision beside the shuttle. These belong to the fresh-from-the-Fleet-Academy Ensign who's responsible for this particular shuttle. She's a qualified officer, for sure, and high-classed as far as assessment letters go, but she still doesn't know the first thing about making older craft like this particular shuttle play nice. The academies train officers with *skills*, sure, but they all train on brand-new systems that haven't seen actual space service.

Luckily for Elias, though, this Ensign Phoenix is the sort of officer who *wants* to be shown how to do the things the Academy branch at Kapteyn didn't have time to teach her. She's been quite pleasant company, in fact, even if she does outrank him. It's worked out well for him that she was in a position to request that he stay an extra day to help sort out her shuttle, too, since that means he has another excuse to be around his favorite pair of officers a bit longer before he has to go back to his own ship.

"So, ma'am," Elias says, continuing his running dialogue with the young officer's legs, "here's that other problem I told you we might find—some of the coils under here are corroded."

"Where?" Ensign Phoenix pokes her pale, close-shaved head up under the shuttle. She still has traces of shimmering non-conductive grease smeared across her cheek from when the two of them replaced the shuttle's main relay power bank this morning.

"It's the primary set here." Elias gestures to the collection of coils with his circuit probe.

"Which ones?"

"Slide under and see if you can spot them." Elias hands her the probe and crawls out so he can stretch for a few minutes and give her more room. "It's the upper part of the coil that's most prone to corroding, but you'll never learn how to see them if you don't look for yourself."

Ensign Phoenix laughs and wriggles into the space he's just vacated. "You're an odd sort of a teacher, Rudy—you know that?"

"Heh. I'm going easy on you, Ma'am. My mum wouldn't have bothered telling you which set had the bloody problem until you'd spent an hour looking for it already. Let me know when you spot them and we can get the lot sorted with replacements."

"Will do!"

Elias leans against the side of the shuttle while the young officer performs her inspection. Granted, Ensign Phoenix isn't *that* much younger than he is—just less experienced. He's been playing with relay tech and old craft since he could walk, thanks to the homestead's flitters and his mum's work as a general mechanic for most of the other farms back home.

He looks out towards the soap-bubble shimmer of the atmosphere containment field over the shuttle bay's doors. The doors have just opened, allowing for an amazing view of the stars stretching beyond the Fleet's cluster of ships. As long as his feet are securely anchored to the floor, Elias genuinely enjoys looking out at the reality of space.

The small craft that lands on the other side of the shuttle bay from the one he's helping repair is of a different make altogether: all stark crystalline angles with an intricate pattern of oil-slick color markings tracing in spirals over every surface. The larger T'irsh-fel ship that it came from is visible outside the shuttle bay doors, floating a few hundred meters away from *Aegolius*. Elias has never seen one of these crafts up close, but if he could he'd be more than happy to dismantle all of their communications systems to try to sort out how humanity's allies do things— not that *that's* ever going to happen.

As far as he knows, the T'irsh-fel are the more adamant of the two allied species when it comes to letting human scientists and engineers anywhere near their technology. From what his Musketeer bunkmate has said about the Prelvee from his time flying with them, they're more of the mind to share small things *subtly* with individual humans on a case-by-case basis even though officially they're not allowed to.

Back on *Surnia*, in his free time Elias is still working on untangling a few of the puzzles the Prelvee mechanics left behind when they put Sarge's poor darter back together after they rescued him from a battle two years ago, too. He's looking forward to meeting those ladies someday, if only to see what they think of how he's incorporated their hints into the other three darters he's responsible for keeping flying.

If humanity's collection of colonized stars didn't happen to sit right in the middle of a fifty-light-year-wide area the Novan Empire needs to control in order to better their chances of conquering the outer territories of the T'irsh-fel-Prelvee Alliance, these more powerful species would probably have waited at least another hundred years before making contact at all. Likewise, though, without the T'irsh-fel and Prelvee intervening as much as they have, humanity would have been overrun almost as soon as the Novans figured out that they existed.

Elias watches with interest as the side of the T'irsh-fel shuttle shimmers and morphs into a staircase leading down from the main opening. *There's* another little technological mystery he'd love to have a chance at unraveling. The T'irsh-fel are known for their way with malleable programmed matter and micro-machines for a reason; even if they haven't gotten to a point of wanting to share their tech with humanity, a little thing like that can't stop a man from wondering how it all works. Dons has told him a bit about the short-range telekinesis they've witnessed, so maybe that has something to do with it. All Elias knows is that being able to just tap a control board and have a darter reassemble itself from a pile of parts would be *far* more convenient than having to weld its wings back on every time one of his pilots manages to knock them off.

Admiral Marvin is the first to step down out of the craft. She's followed closely by a blonde woman Elias assumes is the Coalition Diplomat Dons and Li have told him about. He's been fortunate so far not to have reason to be introduced to her, considering that even *Dons* seems to find her frustrating. Both the suspected diplomat and the Admiral are wearing long insulated ivory coats loosely over their uniforms—and with good reason, considering what Dons has told him about the climate settings on the T'irsh-fel ships.

Elias has nothing but the highest respect for Admiral Marvin, not that he'd ever tell her that. All the same, considering how his previous encounters with her have gone, he's immediately glad that she's not looking in the right direction to see him. Courting her favorite former assistant and protégé is not without its dangers, after all.

There's a conversation of some kind going on between the Admiral and the blond woman and the alien in the long golden cloak who's now standing in the doorway of the T'irsh-fel shuttle. That, Elias assumes, is the pilot. All of the thick, hairy purple feathers amongst their bony scales are slicked back down from their four pairs of eye stalks, save for the boa-like ruff at the back of their "neck" just above the cloak's collar. Elias has heard the species described before as something of a hybrid between a feathered snake and a slug, but that doesn't come close to the reality at all.

Dons is the last to step around the pilot and exit the shuttle, fully bundled up with their arms tucked inside their coat. One of the more colorful scarves out of Li's collection is wrapped over their neck and ears, just like it was when they left to join Admiral Marvin in the shuttle bay after breakfast. Elias wouldn't be surprised if they'll need help getting the scarf unwrapped, considering that he can see the frost that's built up on it from across the room.

There's something in the way his friend is carrying themself that is immediately concerning, but Elias can't quite place what it is.

Dons is stiff and moving slowly, and seems waveringly unsteady as they step over to the Admiral's side. They glance Elias' way briefly and un-tuck one of their lower arms long enough to give him a shivering little wave. He decides it's worth having the Admiral get on his case again to check on them and starts walking that way.

Another moment, and he's *running* over because Dons has just passed out and fallen to the floor.

Elias slides in beside them on the other side from where the Admiral is already kneeling and calling for a medic. "Dons? Can you hear me?" He takes one of their hands. It's unnaturally cold to the touch, even for them.

Dons doesn't respond.

"Where in the *stars* did you come from this time, Mr. Rudolph?" the Admiral asks, clearly startled. "I thought I told you to stay off my ship."

"Ma'am, that hardly bloody matters at the moment, does it?" Elias has other things to worry about. His best friend is still an unconscious heap of shivering limbs on the floor. "Dons? Come back to us. What's wrong?"

Elias sees a flicker of movement under Dons' third eyelid, but that's about it. They're breathing slowly, but it's not regular. He slips a hand under the layers of frost-stiffened scarf and coat collar to find the side of their neck and feel for their pulse. It's there, but equally slow.

Then, all at once, he realizes what must have happened. Dons' skin is like ice, just like their hand, even with all of the clothing that should have been holding their body heat in—or would have, if they were *human* and had enough body heat to spare in the first place.

"Forget the medics—you need to call Li back *now*." Elias doesn't bother looking up at the Admiral. He's too busy unbuttoning Dons' coat so he can get his body closer to theirs when he's ready to pick them up.

"Do you have *any* idea who you're giving orders to,

crewman?" The blond woman stares down at him sharply.

They haven't met before, but Elias has decided now that he doesn't like her. If she's this concerned about the chain of command when someone's life might be in danger, he doesn't *want* to make a good impression on her, for that matter.

"I don't bloody care," he says flatly, still focusing on Dons. They're practically soaked underneath the coat, not from sweat but from the high humidity on the T'irsh-fel ship. All the way through, everything Elias finds is *cold*. He realizes he'll have to get the coat off them altogether, and starts carefully but swiftly working each of their four arms out of the sleeves.

"Admiral, this man is *grievously* insubordinate—"

"Trust me, Ms. Harrington, I'm aware." Elias can almost *hear* the Admiral rolling her eyes, her tone is so dry. It quickly turns concerned again as she focuses her attention back on him. "Now, what are you *doing* here?"

"Trying to get this coat off them, ma'am, what does it bloody look like?"

"Watch your tone—" the blond woman begins to say.

"My tone?!" Elias snaps back. "You think *this* is me being insubordinate? Lady, you have *no* idea how bloody insubordinate I'm cable of being—but if you don't stay out of the way you're liable to find out."

"Mister Rudolph," the Admiral begins, her concerned tone taking on a firm edge. "I know you're Celadon's friend... for *some* reason... but you're no medic—"

"I know what I'm bloody well doing! If that bloody *idiot* you call your physician knew what *he* was doing, he'd never have let you take Dons back to that deathtrap of a ship in the first place." Somewhere in the back of Elias' mind, it dimly registers that he's shouting at the Admiral, and that *can't* be a good idea in the long run. At the moment, he doesn't care.

Elias finally manages to free the last of Dons' limbs from their coat and throws the soggy garment aside. He gently gathers up the tangle of damp, unconscious Florivan and holds them as close as he can while he gets to his feet, taking them up in his arms like a child. Dons barely responds, but their face moves against the side of his neck ever so slightly. He takes that as a sign they might be at least *somewhat* able to feel his warmth.

"And just *what* do you think you're doing, crewman, since you think you're such an expert?" the blond woman hisses.

This is the point where what little patience Elias might have had left completely disappears. There are a number of very good reasons he's not an officer. This sort of nonsense is definitely one of them. "What I'm doing, *ma'am*," he says, dryly, "is taking Dons to their cabin, where I *might* have a chance of getting them warmed up before they're too far gone." Elias glares over at the T'irsh-fel pilot, who's been watching all of this with the same disapproving look the diplomat woman is wearing.

*How dare you!*

A foreign telepathic voice registers in his mind. The tone of it is haughtily offended and self-important; infuriating, in short.

*Have you any idea—*

Elias forces the rest of the T'irsh-fel's telepathic message out of his mind with all the fiery curses and insults he knows formed into one angrily concentrated thought. He doesn't know if the alien can hear or understand it, but at least it drowns out the mental projection of the voice. There's only one line of thought Elias can truly focus on right now, anyway: his best friend is unconscious in his arms, he needs to get them somewhere warmer, and he does *not* have time for any of this nonsense.

"Well you," Elias says aloud, unable to hold the words in, "can tell *your* bloody admiralty that they've got another thing coming if they think that forcing someone who's only halfway warmblooded into a situation where they have to sit in a *bloody freezer* for a week for the sake of bloody battle secrets and showing off how superior you lot are was a good idea." He glances back to the Admiral and the diplomat woman. "Or was that *your* idea? Either way, this was a bloody stupid thing for the lot of you to ask Dons to do to themself."

With that, Elias turns and stalks away, pretending he doesn't hear the cacophony of voices spluttering behind him. When he gets around to the back of the shuttle he was working on before, he stops briefly to knock on the side of it with his foot.

Ensign Phoenix slides out from under the shuttle and looks up at him with wide eyes. As expected, she's been listening to the whole thing.

"Do me a favor, ma'am." Elias lowers his voice and speaks as quickly as he can. "Launch this bird of yours and go over to *Otus*. When you get there, tell Lt. Hsu I said he needs to get his arse back over here so his jumper doesn't finish bloody freezing to death when they drag me to the brig. Can you do that for me?"

"Yeah. Are they going to be okay?"

"I hope so. Now get going."

Ensign Phoenix nods seriously and slides back under the shuttle to close up the access ports. Luckily for all of them, the temporary repairs to the shuttle's close-range communications system *should* hold long enough for her to make the trip to *Otus* and back—with the radio silence orders in effect, though, she shouldn't even need the system at all.

Elias gets all the way down the main corridor to the lift before anyone tries to stop him.

"Mister Rudolph!" shouts the Admiral, coming up behind him. "If you think for one minute you can get away with—"

"Yeah, yeah, I know. You can throw the bloody book at me once Li gets back."

The Admiral catches a hand on his shoulder and locks her eyes onto his. "Are you sure about this?"

"Do you even care?"

The Admiral's eyes narrow. "They're my friend too, mister."

"Then let me help them, *ma'am*." Elias shakes his head and taps the command pad to call for the lift. "I've seen hypothermia in Florivans before—Wyndi's given us a scare or two, believe me. Dons has been coming in chilled to the bone every night since this started. Five or six hours *can't* have been long enough in between for them to have fully warmed up before you took them out into the deep freeze again. If I can get them dried off and warm *now*, they'll have a lot better chance of recovering."

The Admiral pauses and fixes him with a steely, firm

look before turning back towards the shuttle bay. "Fine, then... But if you're wrong about this, the brig is going to be the least of your worries, Mr. Rudolph. Clear?"

"Understood, ma'am."

WHEN TOREVAL AWAKENS, THEY'RE RATHER confused to find that they've been sleeping somewhere familiar and *warm*. There's a nest of soft blankets around them, and a warm human who they're curled up against.

After a moment, Toreval recognizes the smells and softness of the nest. They open their eyes slowly, finding that they are, in fact, in their own quarters aboard *Aegolius*. The wonderfully warm human beside them is unmistakably their Navigator. He's sitting there quietly with one hand tapping at a holoscreen with some star chart or other that he's studying and the other lightly stroking their hair.

Toreval has no idea how they got here. The last thing

they remember is getting on the shuttle to come back from the T'irsh-fel ship and part of a conversation with High Commander Qzvyr during the flight about his people's hospitality codes.

"Li?" Toreval shifts themself slightly to look up at him.

"Hey," he says softly, turning his dark eyes down to meet theirs, "there you are, Val. Feeling better?" Li flicks the holoscreen off and sets the device that was projecting it on the table beside their nest.

"Better?" Toreval's mind is fogged with sleep enough that they have no idea what he's talking about. "Why? What happened?"

"From what I've been told, you passed out when you got back from the T'irsh-fel ship. You've been in torpor for about ten hours now. If you hadn't woken up in another two, I was going to have to resort to letting Dr. Dupree take a look at you."

Toreval allows themself a small grimace. They're not fond of the new physician who's come in to replace *Aegolius'* recently-retired chief medical officer, and Li knows that. Dupree is the sort of medical scientist who is eagerly curious about Florivan anatomy in *entirely* the wrong way, and has been pestering Toreval about personal matters that are none of his business ever since he came aboard.

Their Navigator doesn't exactly like him either. Li doesn't appreciate having to repeatedly turn down passive-aggressive suitors any more than he does having to intervene for Toreval with medical staff who should know better where the lines of privacy have been drawn. If Dr. Dupree weren't so skilled at taking care of the rest of the crew, they'd have already asked Jenny if she'd be willing to do something about him. They still might, once this whole mission is over with and they're back in a port where they could conveniently leave the man.

"Only as a last resort, Val. *Tyto* won't be back from their scouting run until tomorrow, so since we're still under radio silence, calling them up and having Sodalite jump them back early to take care of you wasn't an option." He shakes his head. "The minute they get here, though, they're going to check you over. Admiral's orders."

"Of course..." Toreval sighs softly. At least being examined by a physician who's a fellow Florivan won't come with a lot of uncomfortably eager questions about the nonstandard aspects of their anatomy. "But why was I in torpor at all?"

"I was hoping you could tell *me* that. Elias was thinking hypothermia from one day too many in a place that was too cold for you—I'm inclined to agree with him."

"That's... probably right." Toreval takes a few moments to consider it. That would explain a lot of what they're feeling now, too, especially the aches all through their body and deep in their old scars; those are likely just from being chilled.

"Toreval. You really scared me this time, you know?" Li's using his serious tone—but more than that, he's calling them by their full personal name. Even though they gave him permission to use it years ago, Li usually sticks with the nickname he's given them.

"I didn't mean to scare anyone, Li." Toreval feels almost like a naughty little kitten being scolded for coming home from an adventure injured or chilled. "It just sort of happened."

Li sighs. "We could have done something to prevent this. Why didn't you tell me how badly the cold was getting to you?"

Toreval doesn't answer immediately. "I... I didn't think it'd get this bad, to tell you the truth."

"Really?" Li raises an eyebrow. "I know you're not really a warm-blooded mammal like me, Val, but I'd think *you* of all people would be aware of what your limits are."

Toreval hesitates. He's right. They *should* have known better. "...I may not have been thinking clearly enough after the first day of the talks to recognize the danger."

"Too cold to realize being cold was a problem?"

"That sounds about right, yes." At the moment, though, they're finally starting to feel warm again—for what feels like the first time in ages—and they don't have the energy to process much else. Toreval snuggles in a little closer to Li. He's *warm*, after all, and they're still a bit chilled and achy all over. More than that, they don't often get to do this with him. They share a close friendship with their Navigator, but Li isn't the type of human who likes being cuddled frequently.

"You have to be more careful, Val." Li sighs and resumes the gentle stroking behind their ears. He's no doubt aware that he's liable to put them back to sleep doing that, of course. That calming reflex held over from kittenhood is something he's familiar with; so is the fact that their species is tactile-affectionate by nature and that it's the simplest way to reassure them that he's not going anywhere. "Just... don't scare me like that again any time soon, okay? You were barely even breathing when I got here, even though

Elias had mostly thawed you out by then. I don't think my nerves could take seeing you like that again."

"I'll try not to let myself get talked into being a snowball again. Promise." Toreval finds his unoccupied hand and gives it a gentle squeeze of reassurance. "I'm not going anywhere, Navigator. You're stuck with me."

Li relaxes, finally, letting out a small chuckle. "I'll hold you to that."

Toreval has a small realization, now: their other favorite human isn't here. That's not right. He wouldn't have left— not when Li is here with them and was clearly upset. Not to mention that he's naturally warm, even for a human. They can't imagine Li *letting* him leave if he was the one there trying to thaw them out first. "You said Elias carried me here?"

"Yeah. He was in the shuttle bay when you got back— brought you here and got you dried off and warmed back up while I was on the way. I don't think you'd be recovering at all if he hadn't."

"Where is he?"

Li grimaces. "Down in the brig."

"What?" Toreval's mind is still too fogged to make the connection. "Why?"

"Apparently his temper got the better of him again. I'll be honest, Val, I don't know the whole story. He didn't get a chance to tell me." Li shakes his head lightly. The tone of his voice betrays the fact that Toreval isn't the only person he's worried about today.

"That does sound like Elias... but why send him to the brig for it?" Toreval twitches an ear curiously. "I thought Jenny was finally warming up to him..."

"No one's told me the specifics yet. All I know is that the Ensign who came over to *Otus* to get me was shaken up by whatever happened and didn't want to be the one to tell me about it. The Admiral only let Elias stay with you until I got back, but I didn't have a chance to ask her what was going on either—and, to be fair, I was a bit distracted at the time. Security escorted Elias out right after I arrived and he gave me the rundown on what was going on with you."

"That's not nice of them." Toreval doesn't say it out loud, but they know their Navigator would have been better off having someone to sit and worry with.

"I'm going to talk to the Admiral tomorrow—see if she can be a bit more lenient about whatever's going on since he probably saved your life." Li shakes his head again. "I don't want to think about what would have happened if you'd stayed cold like that any longer..."

"I'm fine now, Li." Toreval stifles a yawn. They still don't have enough energy to think about the bleaker possibilities.

"I'll believe that after Sodalite looks you over and says it."

"Fair enough." Toreval makes a vague gesture towards the end table beside their nest with one hand. "Hand me my pocket-com, will you? I know I need to tell Jenny I'm awake so she'll not worry about me—and that I want my other favorite human back. He can't have done anything *that* serious..."

Li obliges, and within a few minutes, Toreval has their answer. It makes even less sense than they thought it would. "So?"

Toreval passes the little device back to him. "She says we can't have Elias back until I persuade the T'irsh-fel

High Commander not to demand rights to extradite and punish him personally for 'grievous breaches of protocol and etiquette of a most offensive nature'... and that she'll explain everything to both of us in person at breakfast because she's too busy trying to prevent this from becoming a major diplomatic incident."

"Ah." Li sighs softly. He falls silent for a few moments, barely moving save for the hand that's gone back to lightly stroking their hair.

"Don't worry." Toreval gives his free hand a reassuring squeeze. "I'll sort it out, whatever it is. No one's taking my nice warm humans away if I have a say in it. If nothing else works, I can always have you bring Indigo over from *Surnia* once Sodalite gets here so we have proper witnesses... and then sneak down to the brig and formally claim him as my heart's-littermate and a member of my household." They pause, grinning up at their Navigator. They're exhausted, but they already like this idea. "And then call in a favor or two and *poof*! Transferred citizenship and Elias becomes the Council's problem instead of Jenny's, and High Commander Qzvyr will have to wait until this operation is over to go to Procyon and negotiate with *them*, since I'm only the Youngest and I'm technically in exile anyway. If Jenny and I haven't smoothed things over by then, the Eldest will. They're good at that."

Li looks down at them, incredulous. After a moment, he finally cracks a smile. "Well, Val, you must be feeling better if you're already plotting mischief."

"I am." Toreval stifles another yawn. "Cards on the table, though? I'll admit I used up most of my energy coming up with that scheme."

"You can go back to sleep if you need to." Li relaxes, finally, picking his own pocket-com back up. "Now that I know you're out of danger, I might be able to do that myself once I finish going over these charts... Mind if I stay with you for the rest of the night, though? I'm not sure I want to leave you alone just yet."

"My nest is your nest. You know that." Toreval contentedly lets their eyes slip back closed. They do feel better than they have in days, even if they're still exhausted and achy. If Li's in a mood to cuddle with them, they're not about to send him away. He's warm, and his presence is comforting in itself. They just want to sleep in the warmth a while longer.

ELIAS HAS BEEN ALTERNATING BETWEEN DOZING and just staring up at the ceiling from the cot in his holding cell in *Aegolius'* brig for a long time now. The white bulkhead is traced with faint seam lines following the contours of the ship's internal structure. He has the pattern memorized, not that there's any use to that information.

There's nothing much else to do at the moment but stare and try to picture where the various power conduits and air vents must run. Being in administrative confinement is *supposed* to be boring, after all, so one is left with no choice but to contemplate their actions and the resulting consequences. At most, he's allowed to ask the guards to set up reading material on a monitored holoscreen for him.

He hasn't bothered with that today.

Elias isn't used to having time on his hands. Normally, if he's not actively working on something, he's either reading up on his tech development papers or busy helping keep the Florivan kitten who lives with his squadron out of trouble. Even when they're not around, he's developed a hobby of fiddling with some of the spare bits and bobs he carries in his work vest's pockets to make small toys and puzzles. He always keeps a few of those on hand for little Wyndi to chase and unravel when he needs them to be occupied with something other than helping him or borrowing his tools.

He'd be doing that now, if he had anything in his trouser pockets besides a bit of lint to work with. His work vest with all of his tools and collection of odds and ends is back in Li and Dons' quarters, unfortunately. Elias took it off while he was tending to Dons and trying to give them access to as much of his body heat as they could possibly absorb, and he didn't see a point in picking it or his pocket-com up when the security officer came to collect him. Both of them would just be in a box somewhere in the security office right now to keep him from potentially causing trouble for the guards, anyway. That's standard policy; as it is, he'd rather leave his effects with Li than have to fill out the paperwork to get them back.

Thus without his usual distractions, Elias stares up at the ceiling, bored enough to be trying to work through what the internal structure of *Aegolius'* brig section must be. Aside from the times when food is delivered or the Admiral and that annoying diplomat woman come talk through the latest version of how he's to be punished for offending their allies, he hasn't been allowed contact with anyone.

Theoretically, all of this is reasonable on their part and in line with regulations. Elias knows he mouthed off a bit when he was trying to help Dons, and that there are, in fact, consequences for losing one's temper. He'd even say his current situation is acceptable, considering the Admiral's admission that he did the right thing and her assurance that Dons is safe and well now.

Still, how was *he* supposed to know that the T'irsh-fel officer he shouted at in the shuttle bay was actually someone important? In a way, he's glad it was their High Commander; it didn't sit well with him thinking he'd yelled at some innocent pilot who wasn't really at fault for his friend's illness.

As it stands, all Elias can do is let his mind wander and try not to linger too long on the thoughts of how much trouble he's gotten himself into this time, whether Dons is really recovering from their bout of hypothermia, and most of all, how Li must be taking all of this. He would have liked to be there with the two of them until Dons woke up, if only so poor Li wouldn't be left to sit and worry alone. If he had his choice, though, he'd stay by Li's side regardless of whether there was a *reason* to be there.

Elias has lost track of the hours passing when the sound of the keypad outside that controls the outer wall of the cell catches his attention.

"Hello, Elias," says a familiar wind-chime-toned voice as the outer wall to his cell begins to slide open. In a moment, it reveals Dons standing with a security officer he doesn't recognize on the other side of the containment bars.

Dons has one of Li's scarves on again over their standard uniform: the purple one he'd given Li for a birthday gift. He has a suspicion that Li *insisted* they wear it, too, and the usual bit of banter from Dons claiming they don't want to be fussed over and Li being amusedly matter-of-fact about his "Navigator's duty to be concerned for them" must have been adorable. He's annoyed to have missed that.

"Hey, Dons!" Elias sits up and waves to them. "All back to your usual, I see?"

"Yes, thank you." Dons does seem far more like their usual self than when he left them sleeping in their blanket-nest four days ago. It's good to see them awake and moving. Their tail swishes with what he's come to recognize as a mild annoyance. "I would have come to check on you sooner, but—"

"Let me guess, that wonderful Navigator of yours didn't want to let you out of your nice warm quarters until he was sure you'd not take a chill again?"

"You know him too well." Dons stifles a laugh. "Well, that and I've been busy trying to persuade the T'irsh-fel High Commander not to demand to extradite you so he can punish you under their laws for being rude while you were saving my life. We have a bit of a plan to at least get you released into my custody so you don't have to be *here* in the meantime, too, but I won't get to put it into effect until tomorrow... my witnesses are a bit tied up at the moment."

"Ah. Thank you for trying, at least." Elias absently rubs at the back of his head. He's been pointedly trying not to think about the latest news he's been given about his potential punishments under T'irsh-fel law. None of it sounded pleasant.

Dons sets a hand on the panel by the smaller access door. It beeps, and the door opens, allowing them to slip in. The security officer who escorted them shakes his head and then goes back to the other end of the brig where his post is, leaving the two of them alone in the cell.

"May I sit with you?" Dons asks, gesturing vaguely. "Don't tell Li—he worries too much as it is—but I'm still a little shaky standing for too long."

"Of course." Elias nods and pats the cot beside him. "My bunk is your bunk."

"I... wanted to make sure I got to talk to you today," Dons says softly, once they've sat down. "Jenny told me what you did for me. I owe you my life, truly."

"Now, really, Dons." He offers them a reassuring smile. "What else was I supposed to do? You weren't exactly in a place to tell them what was wrong yourself. I'm glad I could be there for you when you needed me—and that you and Indigo made a point of telling me what to do about hypothermic Florivans in the first place back when Sarge brought Wyndi home. Just try not to get yourself frozen like that again, okay?"

"I'll do my best. I don't think Jenny will ever let me back on a T'irsh-fel ship without a nurse watching me at all times, though." Dons' ears twitch softly. "In any case, thank you... and I'm sorry you've ended up in here because of me."

"Heh. Hardly the first time I've run into trouble with the Admiral, Dons."

"...True." Dons chuckles for a moment or two. They're likely remembering the last time they had to persuade someone to let him out of a cell like this for something that was only partly his fault. That wasn't as boring as this, of course. The Musketeers were in the cell *with* him. "I think you may have actually made a good impression on her this time, though," they add.

"Oh, is *that* why she hasn't given me over to be deep-frozen yet?" Elias laughs half-heartedly. "Good to know, but I doubt she's ever going to get to a point where she actually approves of me."

"Perhaps not where Li's concerned—he's almost her son, though. Jenny's even more protective of him than I am, not that she'd ever admit it."

"Well, at least *you* like me, then. If your opinion matters more to him than hers does, I just may have a chance."

Elias notices a touch of a shiver run through Dons and raises his arm lightly to allow them to move closer, where he can give them a bit of his warmth. He knows the brig is probably out of their comfortable temperature zone to begin with, and that they must still be more sensitive to the cold than usual after what they've been through.

Dons snuggles up under his offered arm with a smile. "I do approve of you, you know?"

"I *had* noticed, Dons." Elias gives their shoulder an affectionate squeeze. "So, how's your delightful Navigator holding up, then?"

"He's been focusing his nervous energy from worrying about me into campaigning for you to be pardoned and given a proper commendation for saving my life..." Dons pauses for a moment. Their tail swishes softly with the same affectionate irritation they often show when they know Li's concerns over them are justified. "...And this is the first time he's let me leave his sight since I woke up."

"I *was* a bit surprised that he wasn't with you." Elias chooses not to admit that he's also disappointed by the absence—Dons knows him well enough to be aware of it.

"He would be if he could, believe me. The only reason he's *not* is that it's bug-out day. Our first jump's going to be in half an hour, so he's up in the Nav closet making all of the last-minute corrections to his reference marks right now."

"Oh? Since when does *Li* need to correct anything?" Elias raises an eyebrow. The man has an uncanny ability to memorize starcharts and calculate things in his head, after all.

Dons sighs. "Since Jenny doesn't think I'm up to leading the charge yet and we can't move the timeline back, we're having to change the plan so everyone's marks are relative to *Strix* instead of *Aegolius*. We'll be bringing up the rear of the formation instead, just in case—no use having people taking us for a reference if there's a chance I can't manage the full cycle." Their ears twitch lightly with annoyance. "*I* think they're being overly cautious with me, but when Li and Jenny agree on something like that... well, there's no arguing."

"Oh, I'm sure there isn't." Elias chuckles lightly. "One of these days you two are going to have to explain to me how all of that reference mark stuff works."

"Someday! You'd pick it up fast, I think." Dons smiles up at him and then seems to remember something. "Oh! Speaking of Navigators, Julian's back with us for the next week or so. If we're lucky, you'll be allowed to go back to duty on *Surnia* when he and Mirawynd rejoin the Second."

"Ah, now, there's a bit of good news." Elias doesn't want

to think about the implication that he'll be returning to his own ship in a *darter*, so he focuses on the rest of the information. "How's Sarge and his little pocket-scamp doing, then?"

"Well, I think. They just arrived, so I haven't had time to catch up with him. He'll be coming by after his shift to say hello to you, though. You can thank Mirawynd for that—they were very sweet about pestering Jenny for permission to visit. Apparently they've been searching all over *Surnia* for you for days." Dons lets out a fond giggle.

"Oh, yes, I'm sure they have..." Elias shakes his head. Wyndi is a force of nature sometimes; even the Admiral has trouble saying no to their cuteness. "So I should expect them to be bouncing in here looking for cuddles sooner or later while Sarge gloats all about how *I'm* the one who's gone and landed in the brig this time. Thanks for the warning."

"Well, that's darter pilots for you, I suppose." After a few moments more of comfortable silence, Dons sighs and stands up. "I'd stay longer, but..."

"You've got a Drive Bay to set up for tonight. I get it. Take a good look at the stars for me, will you?"

"I'll be sure to."

"Thanks... and say hello to Li?"

"Of course. I'll bring him by during our mid-shift break, if I can—he's missed you, you know?" One of their upper hands lightly pats his head. Coming from anyone else, that gesture would seem condescending; from Dons, it's just their usual sweet Florivan way of showing affection and trying to be reassuring. "It will be good for him to see you. It always is."

With that, they turn to go.

Just before they get to the door, Elias stands and crosses the small distance to stand next to them. He lightly catches one of their lower hands. They turn around and look up at him, curious.

"Say, Dons… I… well." The words are harder to get out of his mouth than he anticipated. There's something he's been thinking about ever since he had to leave Li behind to watch over them alone. He's had nothing *but* time to think about things since he found himself in this cell. Dons is the closest thing he has to a sibling, and he needs to get it off his chest to them while he has the chance.

"Yes?" The hand he's holding gives his a light, reassuring squeeze.

"If I did ask him about… well, making us official… *When* I ask him. You'll be okay with that?"

"Humans are so peculiar." Dons reaches up to set one of their other cool four-fingered hands against his cheek. "I would never stand in Li's way on a human matter like that, especially in this case. I may not truly understand how and why your species does the things it does… but I *know* he's happier with you in his life than he was before. That's all that matters to me."

"Thanks. I'll… I'll remember that, next time I have a chance to ask him."

"I'll look forward to it. Considering what I know of human customs, though, I should probably warn you," Dons says, taking their hand away. "You might want to talk to him about this in private first? Li gets all sorts of flustered when people just declare a claim on him publicly without warning."

"So you're saying I *shouldn't* jump off a balcony and tell a bunch of important people where to shove it first?" Elias fixes them with a pointed grin. "I mean, I've already done that second part..."

"Oh, I should say *not*—I'm not a good example for you, am I?" Dons stifles a laugh. "I didn't know Li had told you that story."

"Dons." Elias tries not to laugh. "The whole bloody Fleet knows that one by now. I'd heard it from Navy long before I ever crossed paths with you, even."

"Well, they know the jumping part. We don't tell just *anyone* that claiming my Navigator in front of the Council was such a bit of undiscussed spontaneity on my part..." Dons twitches their ears, although he can't quite interpret whether the gesture is one of amusement or embarrassment. "In any case, I suspect Li will agree when you ask. I have no doubt you'll be able to come up with terms he'll find acceptable... or however it is these rituals of yours work."

"Thanks, Dons."

They leave Elias in a far better frame of mind than he's been in, even if he is once again alone in the dull emptiness of his holding cell. If he has to be alone with his thoughts, at least those thoughts have a *direction* now.

Five hours after its departure from the rendezvous point, the Defense Fleet's convoy is in Quantum Space Transit and well on its way towards the uninhabited system where the T'irsh-fel intelligence network is certain the Novan Armada will be waiting for them.

For an operation like this, precision and planning are key to moving safely as a group. Each ship's Navigator is aware before every jump into Quantum Space starts which other ships are going to be placed near their own and who will be using which ships as points of reference during the jump. As long as all of the landmarks line up, the Fleet can skip along without a single ship being misplaced—and without any accidental collisions. With the entire convoy still on radio silence, everything depends on the careful preparations the Navigators have made and their coordination during the jumps. If all goes well and according to plan, the convoy is scheduled to get to its destination in less than a month so they can help the T'irsh-fel take the Armada by surprise.

Pilot-Sergeant Julian Potts is a sandy-haired young man officially assigned as the fourth member of the Second Darter Squadron's Musketeers on SCV *Surnia*. Today, he once again finds himself nowhere near his squadron nor his ship. For this first week of the convoy's journey, Julian is assisting the Admiral's own Nav/Quan team as part of his ongoing training as a future Navigator.

To that end, Julian is aboard the battle cruiser *Aegolius*, sitting in what is affectionately known in the business as a Nav Closet. This small chamber just off a starship's command bridge is where the ship's Navigator does their work collating all of the information from the collection of readouts and star charts on the display screens surrounding them to calculate reference points. Meanwhile, their Florivan counterpart is sealed in the ship's Drive Bay to run the jump through Quantum Space according to the marks the Navigator gives them over their dedicated intercom system.

Julian never set out to become a Navigator. He didn't even bother going to the optional Nav aptitude trials when he was in training at the Fleet base at Teegarden's Star. He's a *pilot* above all else, albeit one with a reputation for ending up in odd situations. Still, as the Fleet's resident Elder and trainer of Navigator candidates, Commander Celadon has been adamant about having Julian cross-trained for Nav ever since the two of them met.

That decision has a lot more to do with the orphaned Florivan kitten he rescued during one of his accidental separations from the rest of his unit than Julian himself. From what Celadon's told him, by the end of all the hitchhiking he and Mirawynd did to get back to the Fleet, the kitten had already deeply imprinted on him. Even Wyndi's great-grandparent, Elder Marine, has agreed that Mirawynd is unlikely to ever accept anyone else for their guardian, let alone their Navigator.

There's no way Julian could really see himself turning his Wyndi down either, so Navigator-in-training he is. When Wyndi's old enough, if they do want him for their counterpart, he'll be ready. In the meantime, he's well on his way to being certified to substitute if any of the Fleet's Navigators fall ill or are otherwise unavailable for their own jumpers.

At the moment, though, that means having to spend his whole duty shift sitting and listening in through his headset while Lt. Hsu calls down coordinates to Celadon. The lesson today consists mostly of trying to keep track of everything the two of them are saying.

"And finally, your Down reference is going to be 5B by 3 and E3; that's *Otus*. You got all that, Celadon?" Lt. Hsu taps his stylus on the holoscreen list in his hand and then tucks it back through the hair-tie holding his high looped ponytail of dark hair in place.

"*I have it, Navigator,*" replies Celadon's voice over the headsets. "*What's my target for this one?*"

"Target point is D3 by 3 and 8. Coming out 600 meters to the lower-left and rear of Down. Seem doable? I have points for a half-skip if you're not feeling up to full distance."

"*No, I think I can manage that. Stand by, I'll let you know when I get us there.*"

"Confirmed, Celadon. Safe journey." After the Lieutenant flips his microphone up out of the way, he takes a sip from his coffee and then looks over to Julian with the barest hint of a smirk. "So, you getting a feel for it yet, Sergeant?"

The two of them share a common social circle, but Lt. Hsu almost always addresses Julian formally. He seems to be like that with just about everyone, though, unless he's *specifically* off duty and making a point of being casual. According to Rudy, it's a habit from working for the Admiral too long, just like keeping the proper officer's tone and bearing at all times when he's working is—even if there's no one there to observe. Julian doesn't mind it, himself; he tends to just match the mannerisms of the people he's with anyway.

"Yes, sir, I think so." Julian nods and takes a sip of his own coffee. "I'm glad I'm not going to have to do this full-time for a few years, though. I don't know if I'll ever be able to stand all the waiting your sort sit around doing."

"Hey, now," Lt. Hsu protests with a light hint of a chuckle. "I have plenty of star charts to keep me busy while I wait."

"You have them all memorized, sir. That's well beyond me."

"Point taken—but I'm sure you'll learn. After all, your little friend there is going to need you sooner or later."

"I think Wyndi's more interested in all of this than I am, to be fair." Julian sets down his mug, patting Wyndi's head with his free hand. As usual, they're perched contentedly on his shoulder, watching everything that's going on around him. The kitten is a perfect miniature of the adults of their species, albeit covered in a coat of soft silver fur and roughly the size of Julian's palm, not counting their tail.

"Well, naturally." Lt. Hsu takes another sip from his iced coffee. "I'm sure if Mirawynd had their way, they'd be down there in the Drive Bay with Celadon—they can feel that we're in Quantum Space, after all. They may not understand yet, but they'll have the instinct for where they belong."

"True. It's a pity that they couldn't take Wyndi along this time, sir... but I can see why they didn't want to risk going off-schedule because of this fuzzy little distraction." Julian knows his little co-pilot likes going jumping with the adult Florivans in their life. According to Celadon, unlike humans and most other life forms, it's actually *good* for Florivan kittens to be exposed to the miasmas of Quantum Space regularly, too. They've assured Julian that the year or so that Wyndi was stuck with him on a series of Prelvee ships trying to get back to the Fleet didn't do the kitten any real harm, but sometimes he can't help but wonder.

The fuzzy distraction in question peers up at him with their three large golden eyes and makes an unimpressed little bell-like squeak.

The Lieutenant shakes his head. "You know, Sergeant, sooner or later they're going to know more than one word. Once they're able to talk to you, you'll regret saying things like that where they can hear."

"Maybe so, sir." Julian reaches down and tickles his ward

under their chin.

Wyndi seems to accept that as an apology and rubs up against his hand, purring lightly.

"Have you given any thought to what you'll name them, once they're old enough?"

"Not yet, sir." Julian shrugs. "I still want to take them to Luyten's Star so Elder Marine can be the one to do the whole naming and presentation thing for them. Wyndi hasn't lost enough of the fuzz yet for me to even think about arranging that, much less a good word for whatever color they're going to end up with."

Wyndi's only just started to shed a bit of the fur around their face and ears, after all. Once they're old enough to lose the rest of it, they'll have the sort of smooth silver-striped blue skin as an adult Florivan, keeping hair only on their head and the tuft of their long prehensile tail. In truth, Julian has a hard time picturing his little counterpart as fully grown, if only because he's always known them as a small silver fluff.

"From what Celadon's told me, the ears are a good indicator." Lt. Hsu reaches over and offers his hand to the kitten.

Wyndi makes a happy little squeak and hops onto the hand, excitedly climbing up the rest of the Lieutenant's arm. They enthusiastically nudge his other hand with their head once they've reached his shoulder so he can reach to scratch the itchy balding spots at the base of their ears.

"Your Mirawynd here looks like their ears will be somewhat of a brighter blue... something like a cerulean or a cobalt, I'd say."

"Their parent was kind of..." Julian gestures vaguely as

he tries to find the right words to describe a person he met only once and briefly. "Well, I didn't know what their name was until Celadon tracked the records down for me, but Iolite was sort of an inky indigo color—darker than *Surnia's* Indigo, though. Elder Marine is kind of the same, from what I've seen when we've chatted over the relays."

"Ah." Lt. Hsu nods. "From what I understand, that doesn't really predict the colors of the kittens as much as you'd think. This little one's ears are a bit like Lapis', actually, now that I think about it."

"Is Lapis one of the jumpers I've not met? Or was that a suggestion for the name?"

"Oh, no, Lapis is Celadon's youngest—the one who's out at the Ranger Academy on Earth." The Lieutenant smiles softly, still attentively scratching Wyndi's ears. "I wouldn't be surprised if Mirawynd here turns out to be a miniature of them in a year or two. They certainly have the sparky curious side in common."

"Ah! That Lapis. I think I've heard you and Celadon mention them before."

"I wouldn't doubt we have. Anyway, if you ever saw Lapis standing next to Celadon, you'd see what I mean. It's hard to tell which of them are closely related at all, if you just go by the colors—it's essentially random, from what I understand."

"How does that even work?"

"I have no idea. You can try asking Celadon sometime if you like—if you can get an answer out of them that's less than five shades of cryptic, let me know." Lt. Hsu stifles a laugh and passes Wyndi back over to Julian. "Here, now, Mirawynd, go back to your guardian. I have work to do."

Wyndi makes a series of unhappy squeaks at being removed from the folds of the soft green scarf that they were in the middle of snuggling under.

"They do like you, sir—and they behave better for you than for anyone else I know." Julian sets the kitten back on his shoulder, patting their head gently to settle them down. "I guess because you're a proper Navigator?" Wyndi's shown a distinct fondness for Lt. Hsu ever since they first encountered him. Whether that's because he's Celadon's Navigator or because he immediately picked up on the way they like to have their ears scratched is anyone's guess. He would never say it out loud, but Julian suspects that the fact the Lieutenant is involved with Wyndi's *other* favorite person to pester for cuddles has more than a bit to do with that fondness too.

"Well, I like them too." Lt. Hsu reaches over and gives Wyndi's ears one last gentle scratch. "But I'd wager the good behavior is because they know I'll have a donut to share with them once the shift is over, as long as they behave tonight. Mirawynd might not be able to talk properly yet, but they're smart. They know I'll honor our deal."

Wyndi perks up at the mention of their favorite variety of pastry. They eagerly swish their tail and focus their eyes on Lt. Hsu, squeaking excitedly.

"Not yet, Mirawynd. Work first, *then* we get our donuts." Lt. Hsu genuinely chuckles this time. "I appreciate what a good and patient kitten you're being tonight."

Wyndi lets out a pointedly dramatic sigh of disappointment, then a soft squeak that seems to be an acknowledgment of the compliment. It's adorable—especially because they would usually keep trying to convince Julian or any of the other members of his squadron to have the snacks *now*.

"You see what I mean, Sergeant?"

"Yes, sir, but I doubt it's just the bribery." Julian grins. "When they let Rudy out of the brig, you need to teach him that trick—he's always on my case about Wyndi being too much of a handful when they're 'helping' him."

"Oh, I've mentioned it." A momentary glimmer of a soft affectionate tone colors the Lieutenant's voice as he turns back to his charts and data readouts. "Elias never believes me when I say how well-behaved Mirawynd is when they're up here."

Wyndi squeaks at both humans again and swishes their tail around dramatically before slipping down inside Julian's jacket and curling up in his shirt pocket. They'll probably go to sleep soon—they usually do, when they've decided the world outside their pocket-nest is no longer of immediate interest. Wyndi's young enough still that they spend a lot of the day napping to begin with.

"To be honest, sir, sometimes *I* don't believe how well-behaved they are for you. I could swear you hypnotize them or something."

"Oh, I wouldn't go so far as to say that, Sergeant." Lt. Hsu glances back to him with a glimmer of amusement in his eyes. "If I could hypnotize Florivans into staying out of trouble, I'd start with—"

The pleasant conversation is shattered by sharp static sounds over the intercom headsets and a muffled groan filtering in underneath it.

Lt. Hsu flips his microphone bar back down. "Celadon, I'm getting a lot of static from your end. Are you okay?"

"*It's nothing, Li, I—Give me a moment to re-center—It's probably nothing—*" Celadon's voice is broken off by a sharper breath, as if they're in pain.

The Lieutenant's entire demeanor becomes serious in an instant. "Celadon? Talk to me. What's wrong?"

The com line is silent except for a distant static roar for several minutes. Lt. Hsu flits between all of his different control panels and systems menus trying to clear up the signal.

Wyndi pops their head back up out of Julian's pocket. "Tarantara?" they ask, looking between both men with an anxious twitch of their ears. Of all the words they could have picked up first, it just *had* to be the darter pilot's distress signal.

"Go back to sleep, Wyndi, it's okay. No tarantaras to worry about just yet." Julian pats the kitten's head reassuringly. For once, Wyndi seems to believe him and ducks back into his pocket. Julian wishes he believed himself so readily. He turns his attention to Lt. Hsu. "Is there anything I can do, sir?"

"I don't know, Sergeant." The Lieutenant taps the activation button on his headset again. "Celadon? Can you hear me now?"

"Li? ...Yes, I still hear you." The static is quieter now, but still present under their voice.

"Cards on the table, Celadon. What's going on?"

"*Do you remember... what Azul told you... about why I owe Rebecca my life twice over?*" Another pained breath punctuates each set of words.

Julian sees a look of startled recognition pass over the Lieutenant's dark eyes, followed by one of urgent concern.

"*Stars*, Val, really? I thought you said you couldn't—"

"*I thought so too. Azul, Sodalite—even the Eldest agreed it was impossible... but apparently... they were all wrong.*"

"Okay." Lt. Hsu pinches the bridge of his nose for a moment and then lets out a breath. "You're *sure* this is happening?"

"Yes, Li, I'm sorry, I—" Celadon breaks off with a sharp breath.

The intercom goes dead silent, static and all.

The Lieutenant turns to Julian, his face gone utterly serious. "Sergeant. I need you to go get the Admiral. *Now.*"

"Sir?"

"Just do it. This is an emergency."

"Yes, sir."

Just as Julian is standing to go, the Lieutenant holds up a hand and stops him before he can open the door. "Sergeant, after you find her..."

ELIAS IS NOT AT ALL FOND OF SLEEPING DURING Quantum Space Transit.

It ranks just under shuttle flight in his list of things to avoid at all costs. He can sleep just fine on a starship that's floating along on its golden solar sails during the day, but he's unfortunate enough to be the sort of person whose sleeping mind is highly sensitive to *whatever* it is that goes on outside a ship that's jumped across the dimensional veil. It always messes with his dreams, making them either painfully vivid or just plain nightmarish. He takes night shifts back on *Surnia* if given the choice just to avoid that.

Fortunately for him, outside of a battle setting, transit cycles are set exclusively for the night shift for safety reasons. A ship can only take so many hours of it at a time, and having the majority of the crew off-duty and sleeping makes them less likely to be exposed to dangerous miasma leaks.

*Most* people, after all, get over any odd sleep effects from Quantum Space Transit after a few months in space.

Elias doesn't have it so bad back on *Surnia*, even on the odd occasion that his pilots or the Fleet's operations have made it impossible for him to keep to his usual nocturnal habits. He shares a cabin with Sarge and Wyndi, after all. The little fuzzy scamp of a Florivan kitten is a handful even when they're trying to be good, but they also always seem to show up in his bunk when he's having one of those transit-induced sleep disturbances. The sensation of the kitten's purring when they curl up on his chest has a way of chasing away even the worst of the nightmares. He's never thought to ask any of the adult Florivans he knows about why that is.

At the moment, though, Elias is still the lone resident of *Aegolius'* brig. He doesn't have anything to do except sleep. That leaves him open to the sort of weird dreams that have now morphed into a nightmare that will no doubt stick with him for *days* even if he doesn't remember any of it.

Running. Lost and looking.

*Somewhere he's not supposed to be, trying to reach a door that won't open.*

*There's not enough time.*

*He's chased, he's pulled forward, he's too far from the door.*

*The corridor stretches on forever, no matter how fast he runs—*

The sound of the door opening jolts him out of the depths of unsettled sleep. The person bolting into the cell and shaking him the rest of the way awake, though, isn't one of Aegolius' security officers. It's one of his pilots. It takes him a moment to remember that this particular pilot is supposed to be on this ship at all.

"Rudy!" Sarge shakes him again. "Come on, wake up already!"

"I'm up, I'm up." Elias throws off the younger man's arm and sits up. "Where's the fire, Sarge? You look like we're under attack."

"Jail break—Lt. Hsu sent me." Sarge takes off the Nav headset he's wearing and thrusts it into Elias' hands. "I talked to the guard, they're letting you out on the Admiral's orders—she hasn't *given* any, but that's what I've told them, so try to play along."

"What in the bloody *stars* are you talking about?"

"I don't really know," Sarge admits, pulling him out of the cell and into the corridor. "Just come on, will you?" As they walk by the security officer and Sarge waves to them in an overly polite way, he adds in a whisper, "The Lieutenant said he wants you outside the Drive Bay with the headset on. That's all he told me—I think Celadon's hurt."

To say Elias is confused by this would be a sincere understatement. For a moment, he thinks he must still be trapped in the alarming nonsense of his nightmares. Still, after the incident that led to him hanging out in the brig in the first place, that's all the explanation he requires.

Dons is in trouble. Li needs his help.

That's more than enough reason to risk getting caught escaping his cell. Besides, what's the Admiral going to do if he *does* get caught, aside from throwing him back in the brig?

Once they're safely in the lift, Elias pulls on the headset. "Okay," he mutters, "let's see if we can get some answers." He taps the button on the side of the headset to turn it on and pulls the microphone bar down. "Li? What's going on?"

*"Elias! Thank the stars. Toreval, can you hear him?"*

*"...Yes, I can... I'm sorry, if I had any way of—"* Dons' voice is faraway and their breathing sounds rough.

*"I know,"* he hears Li say. *"Shh, Elias is going to stay on the com with you now while I get the Admiral up to speed and calculate a new jump-out point. Think you can hold on for us for that long? He'll be down in the antechamber to catch you when it's over."*

Elias still has no idea what's actually happening, but at least he knows what they need from him now. "I'm right here," he says. "Now, does someone want to tell me what's going on?"

*"No time, sweetheart, sorry. I'll explain later."* With that, he hears the click of a microphone switching off and it's just his Florivan friend's voice left on the other end of the intercom.

*"Elias?"*

"Yeah, Dons, I'm here. You sound awful—Sarge said you were hurt?"

*"That's... heh... one way of putting it."* Elias doesn't like the faraway, pained echo in their words at all. He's never heard Dons over the Nav com-link before, though, so he doesn't know how much of the distortion he's hearing is normal for when they're in Quantum Space.

"Okay, I'll save my questions for later. What do you need

me to do?"

"*Just... keep me anchored, for now.*"

"I can do that. And when you jump us out... I'm guessing you're going to need help walking to sick bay?"

"*...No, not—*" Elias is sure he hears an actual groan of pain now, and a sharp intake of breath. "*Not there—can't... don't let anyone examine me. Especially not—it's too dangerous.*"

Elias has no idea how a medical examination could be dangerous, or *who* it would be dangerous for. The tone of Dons' voice tells him this isn't just more of the usual Florivan reluctance to let human doctors or scientists anywhere near them—or, for that matter, their distaste for *Aegolius'* new chief medical officer.

"Okay, then. One ride straight to your quarters, same as last time."

"*...Your voice is warm, you know that? ...Almost as easy to anchor to as Li's.*"

"Okay, no, never thought about it, but thanks?"

There's another long silence. For a moment Elias thinks he hears them muffle a cry of some kind. They must have a hand over the microphone of their earpiece, trying not to show whatever pain it is they're in. He knows Dons has a high pain tolerance—if whatever is going on has *them* in obvious agony, it must be something considerable.

By this time, the two men have reached the antechamber of the Drive Bay. All of the seals around the door separating the Drive Bay proper from the rest of the ship and keeping the miasmas of Quantum Space inside show lights indicating that they're active and intact. Elias leans against the wall beside the door.

"Sarge, you can go up and tell Li I'm in position. I have a

feeling Dons won't want you to see them hurt—well, not if they look as bad as they sound, at any rate. You know how they get."

The Florivan kitten who's now peeking out of Sarge's jacket pocket looks at Elias and gives him a curious little squeak and an excited wave of both of their left hands.

"Sorry, Wyndi," Elias tells them, making a shooing motion towards the corridor, "you need to go with him. I don't have time for cuddles today—I've got someone else to take care of."

"Tarantara?" Wyndi asks, tilting their head curiously towards the door.

"Yeah, some sort of that," Elias agrees. "Now get going."

"Good luck." Sarge makes a point of setting a hand on Wyndi's head to keep them in his pocket as he turns to go.

Once the two of them are gone and the door to the corridor shuts and re-initializes its own secondary seals, Elias turns his attention back to the headset. "Dons, you still there?"

There's another moment or two of silence before he hears their strained voice again. "*...Yes, I'm... I'm still here. Mostly.*"

"Good. I'm just outside the door now. As soon as you jump us out, I'm here."

"*Elias... If... if this doesn't... If I don't...*" They seem almost on the edge of incoherence.

"Easy, now. Slow down and breathe. I can't understand you."

"*Don't tell Li, but I... I don't know if I'm going to... to wake up this time.*" Elias never thought he'd hear them sound so frightened. The tone of their voice is almost as unsettling as the thought they've just suggested.

"Easy, Dons, whatever's going on, I'm here. Li and I have your back—you'll be fine as soon as we get you out of there." Elias does his best to keep his own tone encouraging, but in the back of his mind, he's starting to wonder just how dire this situation actually is.

A long moment passes, and then there's another sharp breath, then another silence.

*"If something happens to me..."* Dons says at last, *"you'll take care of my Navigator?"*

"Celadon." Elias rarely uses their full name, but it feels warranted right now. "Trust me. Nothing's going to happen to you."

*"Please? This is... I don't know... I don't want him to be alone."*

"Yeah. Okay. I'll keep him out of trouble for you. Promise."

Just after he says this, a click sounds from another headset reconnecting.

*"Okay, Toreval, I'm back. Admiral's up to speed, I explained it all to her as best as I could. I'm calculating the safe jump-out point now. Can you handle that?"*

*"...Li? Yes. What's—"* Another sharp, pained intake of breath. *"Where?"*

*"3F by 3 and 1,"* says Li, who seems to be making a great effort to keep his voice calm and reassuring. *"Just a bit past where you took us in. It should be safe for a few days—and it's within range so we can get to the rest of the convoy again when you wake up."*

*"...Point ...confirmed. Jumping out?"*

*"Go ahead, Toreval, we're ready."*

*"...Jumping... now."*

The coms go dead silent.

Elias watches as the center light above the door flashes for a few minutes and then switches entirely from red to green. One by one, all of the other confirmation lights click over to green as well.

"All right, Li," he says over the headset, "I can confirm the return to Normal space and absence of residual miasmas. I'm unsealing the Drive Bay door now."

One by one, Elias taps through the menus on the access panel and flips each of the analog mechanisms to unseal the door. At his old post at the Teegarden shipyards, he'd helped install Quantum Space Drive isolation and Nav/Quan intercom systems on vessels like *Surnia* and *Aegolius*. He's grateful now that he knows enough to not need a guidebook to deal with all of the safety measures and redundancies and what order they're meant to be disabled in to open a Drive Bay from the outside.

When the door finally opens, Elias sees his Florivan friend floating unconscious in the center of the space on the other side. They're illuminated only by the lights on the panels on all the surfaces of the mostly empty room and the star-scape outside the open viewport on the far wall. It's the only viewport on the whole ship that isn't shuttered when the Drive is active; the rest of the ship is kept as a safe, shielded bubble from the effects of Quantum Space, but for reasons no one but the Florivans really understand, the Drive Bay has to be fully immersed in those effects for the system to work.

Elias is immediately glad that he's in the habit of wearing mag-sole boots. Somehow, he'd forgotten until the moment he opened the door that Quantum Space Drive

Engineers work *weightless*. Even with his boots, the sharp transition from one level of artificial gravity to another as he enters the Drive Bay is enough to make his inner ear reel. He does his best to ignore the sensation; this is too important to let the vertigo win.

With the magnets keeping him firmly anchored to the deck plates, Elias makes his way over and carefully takes hold of Dons' unconscious body. They're all curled up into a ball, with even their tail coiled up around the tangle of limbs. Their hair has gotten free of its braids and buns, somehow. The sheer green and ivory ribbons they wear are out of their hair altogether, gripped tightly instead between the fingers of both their upper hands.

Dons doesn't react at all as Elias carries them out into the antechamber and the ship's artificial gravity field pulls them down fully into his arms. Thankfully, unlike the last time he held them like this, they're still their normal level of not-quite-warm to the touch. No shivers, slow but regular breathing, slow but regular pulse: if he didn't know they'd apparently been injured, he'd think they were just asleep.

"Li," he calls up through the headset, "don't worry, I have them. I'm not seeing any injuries, though."

*"I'm on my way down. I'll meet you in our quarters."*

"Got it. Once Dons is safely tucked into that nest of theirs, you're going to explain this, right?"

*"...Yeah, I'll do my best."*

"Good." Elias hears the microphone click off on the other end of the channel and pauses just long enough to flip his own headset up into the off position.

He's encouraged by one thing: as he's carrying them down the corridor, he's holding Dons close enough that he can hear just a hint starting of that purr of theirs. If nothing else, that gives him hope that whatever injury they've suffered isn't too terribly dangerous—more than that, it makes him think they might in some way be aware of what's going on around them, even if they seem unresponsive.

"Well, Dons," he says softly, just in case they can hear him, "looks like I'm carrying you around the ship again. We really need to stop meeting like this, you know? People will talk."

ELIAS IS ONCE AGAIN SITTING IN HIS USUAL SPOT on the couch in the quarters that Li and Dons share. After he helped get the unconscious Florivan tucked into their little blanket nest, he thought it would be better to give Li some space with his counterpart before asking too many questions. That was an hour or so ago.

Surprisingly, no one from Security has come by yet to collect him and take him back to the brig. This suits Elias just fine, but he still doesn't have a clue what's actually going on. He's content to wait for Li to explain. His favorite officers' quarters are a far better place to be sitting and waiting than the cell he's been stuck in. There's even a beverage dispenser in here for acquiring a decent cup of coffee.

When Li does finally emerge from whatever vigil he's been keeping, Elias has a full glass of strong, sweetened black coffee over ice waiting for him too. Personally, he prefers his hot and with nothing more than a bit of milk, as is *proper* for coffee, but he also knows that it's not a good time to tease Li about his odd beverage preferences. They have more important things to talk about.

"Here," Elias says, holding out the glass. "Figured you could use this."

Li takes an appreciative sip from the glass and sighs as he sinks down onto the other end of the couch. "You have no idea how much."

"How's Dons doing, then?"

"They're okay, I think—there's no any sign of complications yet, at least..." Li pauses to take another long drink and then swirls the remainder of the coffee and ice chips around in the glass. "I have no idea how long they'll be in torpor."

"So this *isn't* something left over from last week's little adventure, then?"

"No, not really—well, that might have been why they didn't recognize this was going to happen, but no." Li shrugs vaguely.

"You've been taking cryptic lessons from Dons again, have you?" Elias raises an eyebrow.

"It's hard not to pick that up from them." Li shakes his head and forces a laugh. "I take it you still want that explanation?"

"If I'm allowed to have one, that would be nice," Elias says dryly. He's been around Florivans enough by this point that he knows there are some things one typically *never* gets to hear explained.

"I suppose we sort of owe it to you, by this point." Li sighs and makes himself comfortable on the other end of the couch with one leg tucked up underneath the other, so he's facing Elias.

"All right." Elias finishes off the dregs of his own coffee and sets the empty mug on the end table behind him. "Two questions: what in the bloody *stars* happened to Dons? And why'd you break me out of the brig to help?"

"Oof. Second question's easier. Val trusts you with their life. You're the only person I know who they've got a strong enough imprint on that I could be *sure* they'd be able to anchor onto your voice... and I knew you'd want to help if you could." Li pauses and gestures with his coffee before taking another sip. "And it was less of a jail break and more I asked the Admiral for retroactive permission after I explained everything else to her. You've been officially released into my custody so you can help me watch over Val until this situation's resolved."

"Okay, that's... clear as mud to a point, but I get you." Elias smirks at Li. "Don't worry, I promise I won't try to escape from you, *Lieutenant*."

"Better not, mister." Li makes a halfhearted attempt at a smile. "Val wasn't happy you were gone already when they woke up the last time."

"Oh, is that so?"

"They like having you around. You might have noticed?"

"I might have, yes."

"I asked them what they thought of you once, you know." Li raises an eyebrow to him and takes another sip from his coffee. "I'd thought you'd just be another lovely person I never saw again after our leave was over before you kept just... *manifesting*, like you always seem to, right when I need you—and it surprised me just how quickly Val befriended you."

"...Do I want to ask what they said?"

"If I remember correctly..." Li holds up two fingers from his free hand to make air quotes. "It was something like 'he's a cheeky young scoundrel who doesn't treat me like an Elder, and his voice is warm.'"

"That does sound like Dons." Elias chuckles briefly, then remembers what he was trying to ask. "Before you get all adorably distracting and nostalgic... you were going to tell me what's happened to them."

"Right. I was."

"Starting with why they're in torpor, if it's not the cold?"

"It's sort of a protective instinct, remember: if they're hurt badly enough or sick, they fall into torpor so their body can focus on healing."

"And they're not injured now that I could see. So what's happening?"

"It's an internal wound—and a couple of other things..." Li sighs.

Elias knows Li isn't good at beating around the proverbial bush, which makes him wonder why the man is even *trying* to be vague at all. "Might as well just tell me, Li. I'm not much help to you if I don't know what help you need—and you *know* I'm here for both of you, whatever's going on."

Li seems to relax. He nods. "All right, cards on the table. I need your promise that you won't breathe a word of this to anyone unless Val tells you otherwise."

"You've got it." Elias' curiosity is piqued. He knows there are a lot of things that Florivans only share with their Navigators, but even as one of Celadon's closest friends, he never thought *he'd* learn any of that.

"You know Val's an Elder."

"Never paid much mind to it, really—they don't come across as *old*, you know—but yeah. Why?"

"They didn't get the title because of their age. It actually means something more like 'first of a family.' They're an Elder because they've been through this twice before and survived..." Li pauses to take another sip from his coffee and then shakes his head with a small sigh. "Val's in torpor now because their biology finally caught up with them."

"Meaning...?"

"Meaning, if they survive this, they'll have kittens to show for it when they wake up."

This is probably the furthest thing from any guesses Elias might have had. He's aware Dons has children, of course, although he's never met either of them. He's *certainly* aware of how different the species' kittens are from the adults, too. Wyndi's given him a good education on that point. Somehow, though, he'd never wondered at all where Florivan kittens *came from*.

"That's good, then?" he asks. "Not the best timing, but—wait, *if* they survive?"

Li shakes his head again. "What little I've been told is that everything to do with reproduction for Florivans is incredibly painful and potentially deadly and they have no control at all over when or if it happens... or who it happens *to*. The only reason the Council let Val leave Procyon and volunteer for the Fleet at all was because it was supposed to be impossible for this to happen to them again."

"And it did, and they didn't *know* it was going to?"

"Yeah. The whole hypothermia business covered up any symptoms that could have warned them. Even Sodalite didn't pick up on it when they were here to check on Val the other day—and they're an *expert* on Florivan medicine and biology."

"That explains a lot."

"Again, I don't know the mechanics of it and I'm not sure I ever *want* to know the details. All I was told is that they have to go into the Strange for it to happen and they die if they try to avoid it."

Elias sits there shocked for a moment or two before he finally finds something to say in response. "Nature didn't give them many options, did it?"

"Not really. That's the problem with them being a species that's halfway native to Quantum Space, I suppose. It's easy to forget that Florivans are so... different... when they seem so much like us otherwise. But they are." Li stops to sip at his coffee again, clearly more so he can take a moment to find the right words for what he wants to say. "If Val was anyone else, this would have happened years ago—Lapis had been out of the pouch long enough when we met, at least. If it was going to happen, it *should* have been back on Procyon where someone with experience could have helped them." Li shakes his head sadly. "But even if there was another Elder here who knew exactly what to do for them... Val could *still* die from this."

"But they're not going to, right?" Elias asks, wondering after the question is out whether he should have asked it.

"That's the worst part," Li sighs, staring down into his

coffee now. "I don't know." He falls silent for a long while, absently running his finger around the rim of the glass.

In all the time Elias has spent with Li, he's never seen the man look so utterly defeated—even when the two of them last saw each other and Dons was still in danger from hypothermic shock, Li still had a glint of hope in his eyes.

"Li?" he asks. "Are you okay?"

"...No." Li doesn't look up. "It's all still sinking in... and I can't stand the thought of losing them. If I'd had any clue that this was a possibility, I'd have taken leave from the Fleet months ago and dragged Val's tail back to the Elders *myself*."

"It's that serious, then?"

"Yeah." Li continues staring down into the swirl of his coffee. "It's maybe one in ten or so of them who can have kittens to begin with. Less than that who survive it the first few times it happens to them. The odds... well, they aren't good."

Elias can hardly believe what he's hearing. "How in the bloody *stars* have they not gone extinct?"

Li shrugs. "Enough of them live and those ones have enough kittens to make up the difference, from what I understand. Like I said, I only know pieces of it. Val doesn't like talking about this, you know? Even more than most of them. They were too young when it happened the first time, really—that's what Azul's told me, at least."

"And Azul is...?"

"Val's mentor from *Caleana Major*, back when they did their QSD apprenticeship."

"Ah." Elias nods. "And they said Dons was too young to have kittens?"

"Again, this is on the list of things not to tell anyone without Val's permission—"

"You don't have to tell me if you think they wouldn't want me to know."

"I might as well, I'm telling you everything else." Li gestures with his hands vaguely as he's talking. "See, apparently what's *supposed* to happen is that they get to be oh, forty or so, and if they're going to develop into a reproductive individual, it'll happen *then*, when they're fully grown and can stand a better chance of surviving having all of their internal organs shifted around and remade. According to Azul, even other Elders can't tell who's going to turn out that way until it's already started. They have no way to induce it and no way to stop it from happening, but *if* a Florivan survives the metamorphosis, they end up catching a litter of kittens every ten years or so. Apparently it's supposed to get easier as they get older and learn what to expect... and most of them don't have as high a chance of dying after their second litter."

"Okay... weird, but okay. What's different about Dons, then?"

"They were abnormally young when the metamorphosis hit them—as in not even fully grown yet. Things never really developed quite like they're supposed to... and after their second round almost killed them, the internal scarring was *supposed* to be too bad to let them ever catch a litter again. The other Elders thought that was all done with."

"And it's not?"

"And it's not." Li lets out a frustrated groan. "And we just have to *sit here* and hope that Val wakes up in a few days and everything's right as rain, because since we're having to stay on radio silence... there's no way I can get into contact with Azul or any of the other Elders and ask for advice, or even to Indigo or Sodalite."

Elias shakes his head, almost at a loss for words. It's all too much for him to take in at once, really. He's starting to see, though, why Dons had been so insistent that he be there to take care of their Navigator. "So aside from the kittens themselves... This bloody well sucks, Li, doesn't it?"

"That's the size of it, yeah."

Elias scoots over to Li's end of the couch and offers him a hug.

Li accepts it—and, uncharacteristically, doesn't let go after a few seconds.

"You're really worried about them, aren't you?" Elias asks, settling into a more comfortable position beside him.

"I'd just gotten to a point where I *wasn't* as worried about them from last week, and now..."

"Well," Elias begins, unable to think of something better to say, "at least you're not sitting here alone?"

"Yeah." Li rests his head against Elias' shoulder. "At least there's that."

Soon, Elias is the one sitting beside Dons' unconscious form keeping watch over them. He's not sure if they're aware of his presence or not, but Li has assured him that the extra warmth from someone being close to them should be good for them. The soft sound of their purr is enough for him to believe they must, on some deep instinctive level, be pleased for the company.

Li hasn't been gone long. He was reluctant to leave at all, but as the ship's Navigator, he has the responsibility to double-check that all of the systems connected to the Drive Bay were shut down correctly after the last jump of the night. He said he'd stop at the mess on his way back to get food for the two of them, though.

"Well, Dons," Elias says, absently reaching over to brush

a stray lock of hair out of his unconscious friend's face, "I know you said you had a plan to get me out of the brig... but I doubt this is what you meant."

There's no response, of course, but Elias swears there's a hint of a twitch from one of their ears. He wonders if they can hear him talking, and makes a mental note to ask Li about that later.

"Come back to us soon, okay? That wonderful Navigator of yours is going to end up with an ulcer from worrying about you, at this rate." Elias pauses, shaking his head. "He's not the only one... but don't worry. I'll keep my promise."

A chime at the door to the shared cabin's common area catches Elias' attention. It confuses him for a moment. Li didn't say to expect anyone, and if it was him, why would he bother ringing?

When the first chime turns into an insistent repeated cacophony of them, Elias grimaces and stands. "Just a minute, Dons," he says, tucking the blanket back into place where he was sitting, "I'll be right back."

He's barely halfway across the common area when the door opens on its own. A pale-complexioned middle-aged man wearing a lab coat over his uniform strides in, glowering. They've never met before, but something about the expression on the man's face tells Elias that they're not going to get along—not to mention that he's barged in without permission.

"Where's my patient?" the man demands.

"And you are?" Elias asks dryly, crossing his arms. He has a suspicion that the unannounced visitor is the same new ship's physician that Dons has complained to him about, if only because he can't think of anyone else in *Aegolius'* crew who'd be able to open the door without the resident's personal access code. "Li didn't tell me he was expecting anyone to drop by."

"I could ask *you* the same question, crewman." The presumed Dr. Dupree makes a dismissive gesture and moves to walk around Elias. "Now, where—"

"They're not your patient." Elias steps in front of him. "And I have a feeling Li doesn't know you're here. From what I understand, I doubt he'd want you in his quarters at all."

"He should have called me hours ago!" Dupree huffs. "In any case, the Commander is a member of my crew—"

"—The *Admiral's* crew." Elias rolls his eyes. He's not in a mood to even feign politeness. "And even if *she* bloody well comes down here and orders me to let you in, I'm not letting you anywhere near Dons."

"What makes you think you have the right to get in my way?" Dupree sputters a little. "I'll have you know I'm certified in Florivan medicine—"

"I don't bloody care *what* you're certified in." Elias stands his ground. He's heard more than enough from Dons lately about how uncomfortable this man makes them—and how proud he is of that certification he apparently earned without ever having met a Florivan in person before he joined *Aegolius'* crew. "Dons made it clear they don't want to be probed while they're in torpor. You might as well find someone else to pester until *Li* says you're allowed in here."

"They're properly in torpor?" The look that flashes across the man's face isn't one of concern; more excited curiosity quickly muffled by self-important bluster. "All the more reason you should get out of my way so I can assess their condition—"

"Again, no." Elias once again moves to block his path as he tries to move towards Dons' room. "Dons told me about the last time you tried to give them a physical. The only thing you'll be assessing in here is my boot if you don't get out."

"I don't know who you are or why you're here, crewman," Dupree begins, puffing out his chest and taking a half step forward, "but if you don't back down and watch your mouth, I'll call security and have you put in custody for flagrant insubordination to a superior officer and impeding a doctor in his duties."

"Oh, will you, now? I'm afraid you'll have to ask Li about that too—I'm currently *his* prisoner, from what I'm told." Elias' eyes are drawn to a flicker of motion outside the still-open door as another figure approaches behind the other man. He smirks when he sees who it is. "But believe me, this isn't me being insubordinate. I haven't even lost my bloody temper yet."

"He's *habitually* disagreeable, Dr. Dupree," Admiral Marvin says dryly, now stepping into the cabin. "But I do have to admit that I'm curious why you're here."

"Let himself in." Elias shrugs.

"I'll deal with *you* in a moment, Mr. Rudolph." The Admiral fixes him with an icy glance for a moment, then looks back to the incredibly startled doctor standing in front of her. "Now, is there a problem here, Doctor?"

"Ma'am, this man is *completely* out of line!" Dupree stumbles over his words for a moment before his self-righteous composure returns. "He's prevented me from examining a patient who is *clearly* in need of medical attention."

"I'm aware of Commander Celadon's situation." The Admiral calmly steps around him so that she too is between the doctor and Dons' private chamber. "And it seems that the whole ship knows they've suffered a bit of a relapse of their recent illness now, considering that you don't go on duty for another four or five hours."

"Surely, Admiral, you can see that they should be moved to the infirmary to be monitored—"

"I've spoken to Lt. Hsu about that already." Admiral Marvin holds up a hand. "You'll find if you check Celadon's health records that they have an advance directive filed stating that he has full decision making power for them in the event they're incapacitated. In this case, he has made it clear that they are to be kept here and not examined by any of the medical staff or otherwise interfered with. I *will* inform you myself if that changes. Is that understood, Dr. Dupree?"

"But—" the protest dies before Dupree can even finish forming the sentence. He apparently isn't immune to the power of the Admiral's tone of unquestionable authority. "Yes, Ma'am."

"Good. You're dismissed. I'll discuss your regular report with you in the morning." With that and a nod in the direction of the door to the corridor, she turns her eyes back to Elias. "At the moment, I have an unruly crewman to deal with."

Dupree makes a hasty exit. As the door shuts behind him, Elias lets out a small laugh. "Well, if nothing else, ma'am, you have bloody good timing."

"I usually do." She rests her hands on her hips. "I'm surprised, though, Mr. Rudolph. It seems you *are* able to control your temper to some extent."

"I'll take that as a compliment." Elias rolls his eyes. "Don't expect me to hold back if he tries barging in again. I don't like that one any more than Dons does, now that I've met him."

"I'll have Security keep your cell warm." Her tone is dry, but there's a hint of a teasing humor behind it. It only lasts for a moment, though. She pauses and looks Elias over for a moment as if she's trying to read his mind. "Celadon really does have a problem with Dr. Dupree, then? Beyond the current situation."

"They haven't told you?"

"I've suspected it, but no. They've made a point of not saying *anything* about him to me since he came aboard. Neither has Lt. Hsu." She shakes her head. "I've worked with them both long enough to know that there's a reason for that somewhere."

"You'll have to ask Dons when they wake up." Elias shrugs. "Or Li, once he's in a better frame of mind. It's not my story to tell. All I can say is that he's too bloody keen on invading their privacy on every level."

"Noted." The Admiral clucks her tongue softly. "I'll have to look into that."

In the silence that follows, Elias goes over to the beverage dispenser. "So, assuming you're here for a social call and not just out haunting the corridors... how do you take your coffee?"

"I don't, this time of night." She seems surprised by the

offer. "Although I did stop by to check on Celadon now that I've made sure the rest of *Aegolius* is still as it should be."

"Figured that. Something else, then?" Elias dimly remembers now Li telling him that the Admiral is the odd sort of commanding officer who wakes up in the middle of the night *specifically* to make the rounds of all the different departments and important parts of her ship and ensure that the night shift is running smoothly. Tonight, of course, she'd have had to get up earlier so Li could give her the rundown on what was happening with Dons.

"No, but thank you." She waves a hand absently. "How are they, then?"

"Dons? Unconscious and tucked into their nest." Elias gets a cup of coffee for himself anyway. "Li said they're about as well as can be expected, for the moment."

"I take it he's told you everything?"

He nods. "As much as I needed to know."

"Including the fact that this cabin needs to have its isolation seals and air filters active as much as possible until Celadon comes out of torpor?" The Admiral raises an eyebrow.

"I know Li put them on before he left, but he didn't say why." Elias tries not to show how much that question caught him off guard.

"Just a precaution—same reason we can't allow Dr. Dupree or anyone else to examine them. The last thing we need is a major miasma leak when the only person we have who could properly deal with it is out of commission." Admiral Marvin goes over to the wall panel by the door and begins tapping at it. "You'll see Lt. Hsu before I do,

I'm sure. Tell him I've deactivated all of the access and override codes to this door except for his. If anyone else tries to get in, I'll be notified."

"Will do." Elias watches her curiously. "Miasma leak risk?"

"Apparently so," she replies. "From what Lt. Hsu said, they're holding a bit of Quantum Space *inside* their body for the kittens. I honestly don't want to know why or how that works. I've had too many secrets about Florivans explained to me for one night."

"Ah." Elias has the notion Dons would be proud of the Admiral right now. Her explanation was just as cryptic as they usually are about things—he has far more questions now that he's not asking than he did before. "All the more reason it's me and Li watching over them, then."

Having finished her task, the Admiral turns back to Elias. "Lt. Hsu, yes. He's the only human I've ever heard of who shrugs off miasma exposure with nothing more than a hangover. You?" She shakes her head lightly. "I have no idea what exposure would do to you—or, for that matter, why you're here."

"I'm here for Li and Dons, ma'am," Elias says solemnly. "You should know that by now. Miasma risk or not, I'm staying."

The Admiral doesn't say anything in response. Instead, she just looks at him for a moment with that sharply focused assessing gaze, then gives the barest hint of a nod. "I'm going to sit with Celadon for a few minutes before I go."

Elias takes a sip from his coffee. "Not going to stop you—Li should be back soon if you want to wait for him."

"I might." She slips through the door to Dons' bedroom,

leaving Elias alone in the common area.

He settles in on the couch and then pulls out his pocket com to send a brief ping to Li to let him know they have company. He can't deny that the Admiral confuses him sometimes. It's a bit eerie, even, to see those rare glimpses of the sense of humor Li and Dons insist she has. Elias doesn't encounter her often enough to really believe them. He's usually at odds with her whenever they run into each other, though, even when he's not trying to be. He's bad at holding his tongue and his temper around authority figures, after all, and she clearly disapproves of his relationship with her Nav/Quan team because of that. It's decidedly *odd* that she's something resembling cordial towards him tonight.

Still, if nothing else, he knows now that she truly does care about Dons. It was written all over her face that she's just as worried as he and Li are. That alone is enough for him to mentally call a truce with her for now. Better to wait to continue his game of annoying the Admiral until Dons is awake to intervene when she gets to the point of wanting him removed from her ship.

A WEEK PASSES, AND THE CONVOY HASN'T SENT any ships back looking for them. That's to be expected, though, with the whole mission being far more important than one ship falling behind—even if it happens to be their Admiral's flagship.

As far as the majority of the crew knows, *Aegolius'* jumper has just had a relapse of their recent cold-induced illness and will be right as rain in a few more days. The handful of people who *do* know anything about what's really happening are all on edge, facing the possibility that Celadon Toreval might never wake up at all.

Julian Potts is one of that handful, although he's only been given the highlights of an explanation. He's not sure Lt. Hsu would have brought him into the circle at all, except for the fact that he's Wyndi's guardian. Julian already knew more about Florivan kittens and where they come from than even most Navigators, after all. More than that, because of the circumstances under which Wyndi came to be his copilot, he's also the only other person aboard *Aegolius* who's survived a significant miasma exposure.

Julian doesn't really remember that incident, but Celadon and Indigo have agreed that it *must* have happened, or else nothing about how he and Wyndi wound up floating in a crippled darter three light-years away from where they should have been makes sense. Their theory for why he survived and had no noticeable ill effects from the experience, naturally, is to do with Wyndi. Florivan kittens, it turns out, naturally absorb and dissipate any lingering Quantum Space miasmas around them.

That little bit of trivia is why Julian's spent a good portion of the last week hanging out in the quarters of *Aegolius'* Nav/Quan team. Mostly, he's been either losing card games or studying Nav tech stuff with Rudy and the Lieutenant while Wyndi bounces around the sitting area. The kitten is technically the one on duty here, even if it's just a precaution. The Admiral had made a point of asking *Wyndi* to guard the room, and as usual, they've taken that adorably seriously. Wyndi even hops up onto her shoulder whenever they see her to excitedly squeak what Julian assumes is their report.

At the moment, Wyndi is sleeping curled up in a contentedly purring ball on Lt. Hsu's lap while he runs Julian through yet another set of star-chart diagrams and scenarios. They seem to be a bit concerned about him tonight, considering that they've been insisting on sitting with him specifically even more than they usually do. Julian's used to his little counterpart's fondness for Lt. Hsu, of course, but something about the way they're behaving is different.

Thankfully, the Lieutenant doesn't seem to mind.

Rudy, meanwhile, is off in the other room sitting with Celadon. Either he or Lt. Hsu usually is, at least when Julian's been there with them. He's picked up on how worried both of them are; the Lieutenant is worse at hiding it. Drilling Julian on Nav stuff seems to be a passable distraction for him.

"So, now that you've looked at the charts," Lt. Hsu begins, absently rubbing Wyndi's ears with one hand while he's tapping on the holoscreen in front of him with the other. "The next scenario has you making a full-distance jump to rendezvous with a Fleet carrier—we'll say *Surnia*, since you know her best—and then a half-skip in tandem with her to the coordinates I highlighted. Assume you're taking point on that. Now, what marks do you pass along to Lt. Malarius at the rendezvous?"

Julian scrambles to tap through his notes. "I... give her Entry and Exit marks, right?"

"Which are?"

"Ah..." It takes Julian several minutes of re-reading the charts and running the coordinates he needs through a Florivan Hexadecimal Code conversion matrix to find the answer the Lieutenant wants. "I give her E3 by 7 and A9 for Entry, and then E3 by 6 and A7 for Exit," he says, finally.

"Close."

Julian sighs lightly. "Which one did I convert wrong this

time?"

"You have the right codes for your marks, actually. You just left one piece of information out."

Julian looks through his notes again. "What was that? I thought tandems just needed the right jump-outs—isn't the other Navigator going to calculate all of their own points around that anyway?"

"Yes, but you're still thinking like a pilot."

"I *am* a pilot," Julian responds reflexively. "I can't exactly turn that off, sir."

"No, but you can build on it." The Lieutenant gives him a knowing look. "Now, think like a Navigator, Sergeant. What else do the jumpers need to know?"

"I..." Julian shakes his head. "I can't think anything else for tandems, even though I know there *has* to be something."

"And *this*, Li," says Rudy's voice from the doorway to Celadon's bedchamber, "is why the man's had me reconstructing the tips of his wings twice already this month. It's not a concept he's good with even when he *is* thinking like a bloody pilot."

Somehow, Rudy's grousing is exactly what Julian needed to jog his memory. He lightly sets a hand over his face. "Oh! That's it—I'd give Lt. Malarius the same safe proximity distance as I'd be calling down to Wyndi so they and Indigo can keep the ships from running into each other on the jump-out."

The Lieutenant nods. "Correct, and I dare say you'd have remembered it even if you weren't prompted." He looks over to Rudy with a small but affectionate smile. "Be careful, I'll start training *you* for Nav too if you keep interfering with the Sergeant's lessons."

"At this rate, I'll pick it all up by osmosis." Rudy stretches some apparent stiffness out of his arms, then crosses them and leans against the open doorway. "Think you can manage to teach him not to run into things in his darter while you're on the subject of not crashing starships? He actually seems to listen to you."

Julian rolls his eyes. "I keep telling you, that last clipped wing wasn't my fault—that striker ran into *me*—"

"And you just *happened* to cross into Toussaint's line of fire at the time, so what the bloody striker missed, she didn't," Rudy says in his usual caustically dry way. For reasons he can't quite explain, *this* is the man Julian genuinely considers his best friend: the Fleet's best and most notoriously surly mechanic. "You're going to have to do better than that if you ever expect to be responsible for anything bigger than a darter, Sarge."

Julian's plan for a witty retort is interrupted by a chime from the cabin door.

"Elias, would you see who that is?" The Lieutenant looks down at the purring ball of Wyndi in his lap. "I seem to be the prisoner of a sleeping kitten."

"Lucky kitten." Rudy chuckles and goes to answer the door. "Do I get to deck that bloody doctor this time if he's decided to come back?"

Julian takes the opportunity to set his notes aside. "If we're brawling with *him*, count me in." He doesn't particularly like *Aegolius'* new chief medical officer himself. Rather, *Wyndi* doesn't like Dr. Dupree because he keeps trying to pick them up like they're a laboratory specimen instead of a person every time he encounters them. Julian takes his role as their guardian and protector seriously, so if Wyndi doesn't like someone, neither does he. Also, the man is a bit of a pompous jerk to begin with.

"I'll think about it." The Lieutenant shows a tinge of a smirk. "You realize this is why the Admiral calls you a bad influence, don't you?"

"I never claimed I wasn't." Rudy looks up from the door's control pad. "Looks like we have a friendly visitor, for once. Says he brought coffee, at least."

Lt. Hsu lets out a hint of a chuckle. "By all means, let the coffee in."

Within moments, the door has slid open long enough to allow Colonel Hannemann, the head of *Aegolius'* own First Darter Squadron, to slip in. He's carrying a tray with four lidded mugs and a napkin-covered basket. As usual when he's off-duty, the Colonel has his pilot's uniform jacket loosely slung over one shoulder, revealing the vast array of freckles trailing down both of his tanned arms.

"Evening, gents!" The Colonel calls, "Figured you could use something better than the standard coffee concentrate—I had Hank brew up some of my own stock. You two stowaways will have to doctor it up yourselves, though." He laughs as he places one mug in Rudy's hands. "I couldn't remember how you take the stuff."

"Much obliged, Colonel." Rudy pauses to tap at the door's control pad with his free hand for a moment. There's a subtle whooshing sound as the cabin's atmospheric safety seals re-engage. "What's in the basket?"

"Well now!" Hannemann makes his way towards the sitting area to join Julian and Lt. Hsu. "As it happens, Hank was just putting out a batch of donuts when I got to the mess hall—"

The Colonel is interrupted by a silver flash of eagerly squeaking Florivan kitten shooting up from Lt. Hsu's lap and landing on his shoulder in three short bounces. They hug Hannemann's neck and then excitedly climb down his arm to sit on the tray and inspect the basket in question. Their tail swishes rapidly as they pat at the napkin covering it with one of their upper hands.

"And I knew someone here would be sorely disappointed if I didn't bring them one," Hannemann finishes, grinning broadly. He sets the tray down on the coffee table, then lifts the napkin off the basket and pats Wyndi on the head. "There you go, Squeaks—don't worry, there's nothing in there that you can't have."

Wyndi makes a happy trilling sound and takes hold of the top donut. They pull their prize out of the basket. It's almost the same size as they are, so it takes a few moments to accomplish this. Once they've managed to haul it over the edge of the basket and get a grip on it, Wyndi enthusiastically hops back over to Lt. Hsu's lap. There, they hold up the donut to him in triumph and squeak proudly.

"Yes, Mirawynd, I see you've brought me a donut." The Lieutenant smiles and accepts the offered donut. With the eagerly tail-swishing kitten watching intently, he breaks it in half and holds the two portions back out to them. "Which half do you want?"

Wyndi claims the slightly smaller half, then makes themself comfortable and begins nibbling at it. Where this little ritual of insisting on sharing their donuts with Lt. Hsu—and *only* him—came from, Julian doesn't know.

That doesn't make it any less adorable to watch.

Julian stifles a laugh. "You're going to spoil them rotten if you keep this up, Colonel." He accepts the coffee mug the Colonel had brought for him and pops the lid off. The smell of the steam is strong in the best way; a far cry from the artificial note that some of the coffee concentrates he's encountered carry, for sure.

"As if the Musketeers haven't done that already?" Hannemann laughs. "Consider it part of my prerogative as an officer and one of Wyndi's quasi-uncles."

Rudy comes back from adjusting his coffee at the cabin's beverage dispenser and leans over the back of the couch where Lt. Hsu and Wyndi are sitting. "Have we been keeping count of how many of those they have?"

The Lieutenant shrugs. "About as many as there are folks in the Fleet who Celadon's practically adopted, I'd say."

"Sounds about right," says Julian. "I need to ask Celadon when they wake up if kittens are designed to make everyone around them want to spoil them, really. Even the Prelvee we've flown with tried to do that."

"Speaking of our favorite Elder..." Hannemann glances towards the door to Celadon's bedchamber. "Any news on that front today?"

Lt. Hsu's eyes focus down on the kitten in his lap. His free hand lightly moves to stroke their ears for a moment. "Not yet—no changes really since you came by to check on them yesterday."

Rudy sets a hand on the Lieutenant's shoulder. "Dons will be up causing chaos sooner or later, though. *That*, I'm sure of."

"Of course they will." Hannemann's characteristic

boisterousness falls a touch flat as he says this. "Mind if I sit with your counterpart for a bit, then, Hsu? I had a feeling you boys could use a donut break and another warm body."

Lt. Hsu makes a vague gesture towards Celadon's door. "Go ahead—let me know if they seem to be waking up."

"Will do." The Colonel rises and heads that way.

Rudy follows him. "Just let me grab my pocket-com before you settle in—I was reading some tech notes to them earlier for a little project I've been working on..."

Once both of them have disappeared through the doorway, Julian retrieves a donut for himself and settles back into his chair. Not two seconds later, he feels a small tapping on his arm. Looking down, he sees the eagerly expectant face of Wyndi staring back up at him. They squeak hopefully and swish their tail to match.

Julian shakes his head. "Fine, fine—you're a regular fuzzy little bottomless pit, Wyndi. You know that?" He makes a show of breaking off a chunk of his donut and holding it out to them. "There you go, donut taxes paid."

Wyndi gives him one of their cute little squeaks of gratitude and takes the bit of donut. Within moments, they've scampered back over to Lt. Hsu's lap. The Lieutenant doesn't seem to have noticed that they ever left. He's too focused on staring at the ice cubes he's stirring around in his coffee.

"So, sir," Julian begins, pausing to take a sip from his own mug, "we were going over coordinate selection protocols next, right?" He has the distinct impression that the other man needs to be distracted from whatever he's thinking about.

"Ah, yes, we were." The Lieutenant pulls the star charts

back up on his holoscreen and then turns it so Julian can read all of the text clearly. He points at a specific spot on the chart. "Now, if you're here and your task for the shift is to get the ship *here*..."

Eᴸᴵᴬˢ ʜᴀˢ ɴᴇᴠᴇʀ ʙᴇᴇɴ ᴋɴᴏᴡɴ ᴀˢ ᴀ ᴘᴀᴛɪᴇɴᴛ man. With the way the last week has gone, any small amount of that virtue he might possess has been thoroughly exhausted.

Li had told him that a Florivan parent normally remains in torpor for three or four days after catching kittens. It's been a full week, now, and poor Dons hasn't so much as stirred. The only good sign from them is the soft purring sound they make whenever Li or Elias is sitting vigil at their side. There's a pallor of weakness growing about them, even so, and they've started to lose their body heat again.

Without knowing what to do, their Navigator's only option is to wait and try to keep them warm.

For Elias, though, watching over Li as much as he is over his Florivan friend, waiting isn't enough. It never was. Even on that first night when he carried Dons back from the Drive Bay and Li explained things to him, his mind was occupied with trying to unravel the puzzle that had been laid before him. There are people out there who would understand what's really going on with his best friend and what to do about it. The only question is *how* to get through to one of the spacefaring Elders without the Novan Armada being able to trace the signal.

Now that there's clearly something that's gone wrong, Elias is glad he didn't wait to try his hand at that puzzle until those typical four days had passed. As it stands, he has enough of a working theory to make an attempt at solving it. That's all he needs.

Thankfully, he isn't the only impatient man aboard *Aegolius*.

"So," Elias asks as casually as he can once the door to Dons' bedroom closes and he's sure Li won't overhear, "any chance you owe us a favor I can call in?"

Hannemann takes the chair beside Dons' nest and lays his hand on one of theirs. After a moment, he looks up at Elias and raises an eyebrow. "'Us' meaning Celadon and Lt. Hsu, or the Musketeers? It'd be a stretch to say you could claim one on your own—but I think you know that."

"Whichever one you like. You can put it on Dr. Navy's tab, even." Elias shrugs. He expected this sort of response; darter pilots take the business of favors even more seriously than the average spacefarer. They're not that unlike his grandmother's clan in that way, really. "Whatever mark I can call in, I'll bloody well take it. I'd owe you double if not—but either way, I need your help."

"What's the favor?" Hannemann's tone shifts to one of unabashed curiosity.

Elias picks up his pocket-com from the side table and pulls up a section of the diagrams he's been working through all week. He nudges the holoscreen over where the other man can see them. "I need access to Sarge's darter for a few hours... and then I need you to get him flying long enough that he can do what he and Wyndi do best."

"Which is...?"

"Getting lost."

Hannemann looks over the diagrams for a few moments, then back up to Elias. "I can't say Zöe ever managed to teach me to read comms tech nonsense beyond what I'd need to send a few tarantaras her way if I crashed somewhere the base's scanners couldn't see me easy... but considering the reputation Potts has? I can't imagine it's hard to misplace him."

Elias turns the holoscreen back off. "Trust me," he quips, "it's not hard at all."

"Well, then," says Hannemann, catching just the edge of a grin, "if you can manage to get those repairs his darter *clearly* needs done before I take my boys out to patrol and practice our radio-silent combat maneuvers tonight, I'd say we might have room for a wayward Musketeer to join us."

"I'm sure he'll be glad to be flying again." Elias nods.

"I'll clear it up with your warden and Security before I leave so you can come down to the darter bay under my watch." Hannemann chuckles softly. "Even the Admiral knows how territorial you mechanics get about the darters you work on—I'd never dream of asking Quince to go near Potts' bird, naturally."

"Naturally."

"Fine, then. Give me ten minutes and I'll sort it out." Hannemann pauses, raising an eyebrow again. "We're keeping radio silence on this too?"

"I'd prefer it. Li has enough he's worried about as it is."

"Noted."

Elias hasn't worked with the man much, but he can certainly see now why his old boss back at the shipyards always called Hannemann her favorite co-conspirator. The Colonel picked up everything he needed to, and doesn't seem interested in further explanations.

Elias, for his part, isn't interested in telling Hannemann any more than he absolutely has to. If his plan fails, he doesn't want the Admiral's wrath descending on anyone else.

Not half an hour later, Elias has finally persuaded Li to get some rest while he deals with the Colonel's supposed "urgent maintenance issue." He leaves his favorite Navigator tucked into the nest of blankets beside his counterpart with a promise that he'll be back soon.

Leaving the two of them alone is harder than Elias expected, but it's necessary.

Now, with the First Squadron on standby for their patrol until one last broken darter can be repaired and full access to his tools and the resources of *Aegolius'* main darter bay, everything is falling into place. There's only one person Elias needs to pull off what he's planning to do: the pilot of said "broken" darter.

Elias hasn't told Sarge much, beyond his part in the plan. Luckily, the man has enough understanding of Dons' situation to go along with it. If anything, he seems happy to be able to escape his Navigator lessons for a few hours—not that understanding most of what's going on means that Sarge ever runs out of *other* questions to ask.

"The Admiral doesn't know we're doing this, does she?"

Elias is underneath the darter with most of his body squirmed into one of its lower access ports when he's asked this. His plan, unfortunately, involves carefully rewiring the entire communications system and replacing all of the small fighter craft's relay crystals and connections.

"No, and don't *you* go telling anyone either. If this goes pear-shaped, I'm the one taking the fall for it. Got me? I lied to you and said we had orders to do this—that's all you have to tell them."

"I got you, Rudy. I'm with you, don't worry."

"Oh, I know you are."

"So. You really think this will work?"

"I don't think we have much of a bloody choice *but* for it to work, Sarge." Elias pauses, patting around in his vest pockets trying to locate the tool he needs. "You haven't happened to see my micro-spanner, have you?"

"The round one or the flat one?"

"Flat."

Potts chuckles. "Yeah, I found it."

Elias holds out his hand from the access port's opening. Within a few moments, the small silver-furred form of Wyndi climbs up his arm and onto his shoulder. They deposit the missing tool in its proper place in his vest pocket with a very pleased little squeak.

"Ah. So *you* borrowed it again, did you?" Elias rolls his eyes and takes the micro-spanner back out of the pocket so he can deal with the stubborn relay circuit crystals he's trying to extract. "Thanks, Wyndi. Now stay out of my way, will you? I don't want to zap your tail again."

The kitten may or may not actually understand what he's saying, but their goal was always, apparently, to have an excuse to crawl under his uniform vest and into one of its larger inner pockets.

"Ah, really?" Elias shakes that side of his vest with his free hand. "I don't have *time* for this nonsense."

Potts reaches a hand up and taps on the side of the access port's opening. "Come on, Wyndi, you know better than to bother him while he's working—Sorry, Rudy, you know how they get... I think they've still not gotten over you being gone last week."

"I missed them too, Sarge, but this is a bit ridiculous."

The kitten seems determined to stay right where they are, refusing to be removed from the pocket they've chosen. They bat Elias' hand away and make a pointed series of squeaks before transitioning into their usual contented purring sound as they curl up and settle down for a nap in the bottom of the pocket.

"Oh, you're a bloody adorable menace, Wyndi, that's what you are," Elias says, still a bit exasperated. "It's fine, Sarge. I'm starting to get used to being everyone's favorite heat source. As long as they don't take any more of my tools, Wyndi can stay where they are until I'm done with these circuits—but you're taking them back once we're done here."

"I did apologize for the tool borrowing thing, didn't I?"

"Yes, you did. Doesn't make them any less of a fuzzy little magpie." Elias goes back to his work, kitten purring away victoriously under his vest. "Now, get your arse back up in the cockpit and tell me what the bloody readouts are saying now."

After a few moments, Potts calls back down to him. "It's all looking clear. Your scramble matrix is loading up, too."

"Good. Just a few more subsystems to re-route, and then you can take your little pocket thief and get out there so we can see if my plan's going to work."

Elias gets back to extracting circuit crystals. He's not sure why, but he has the distinct impression that they're running low on time.

Once the reconfigured darter is successfully launched out into the void, Elias quietly returns to the quarters he's *technically* not supposed to have left in the first place. He finds Li still right where he left him in the blanket nest—although awake now and sitting up rather than peacefully sleeping next to Dons. From the look of it, he's been re-braiding their hair again so it's out of their face.

"How are they doing, Li?"

"...Still the same." Li gestures vaguely. "I don't know what, but *something's* wrong. They should have been awake by now."

"All right, then." Elias nods and then holds out one of the Nav-com headsets he's modified to run off the scrambled signals from the darter. "Here. Put this on. We're all set to dial up an Elder for you."

"...Do I want to know what you've done?"

"No, you're better off being able to honestly say you

weren't involved."

"Elias..." Li seems like he's going to say something more, but then sighs and puts the headset on. "Thank you."

Elias slips his own modified headset on and taps the interface of the pocket-com he's rebuilt to run this whole operation without using any of *Aegolius'* systems. "You can thank me once Dons is back on their feet."

ALMOST EIGHT HOURS AFTER HE LAUNCHED, Julian is still pushing his darter at full speed away from *Aegolius* on a trajectory that could, in a few hundred thousand years, put him somewhere near the Centauri Triad. The goal isn't for him to reach any particular destination, though; just to get far enough out that if the signal he's broadcasting is intercepted by someone unfriendly, he won't be close enough to the silent ship he's come from for it to be spotted too.

"This is Pilot-Sergeant Julian Potts of SCV *Surnia* calling any ship within range of my signal," he says over his modified com relay again, "please respond if you can hear me."

His little Florivan copilot is sitting on his shoulder

looking out at the stars, just like they have been since they woke up and emerged from his pocket. Wyndi makes a little bell-like squeak, as if questioning why he keeps repeating the hail. He gives them a brief scratch behind their ears.

"Yeah, Wyndi, I know. We're back in the stars again. But we're on a mission, remember?"

The Florivan kitten just keeps looking out at all the little points of light outside the reinforced poly-glass canopy of the darter's cockpit.

Potts repeats the hail again and checks his fuel gauges. He has an alert set to let him know when he's down to half so he can cut the engines and let the darter keep flying on its own momentum with enough fuel to spare for the trip back to *Aegolius*, but he still keeps checking the gauges out of habit. Emergency or not, he's not planning on getting stranded in the void again today.

*"Really, Lyn, I—sworn I heard another voice—"* The characteristically wind-chime-toned Florivan voice he hears coming in over his headset is a little static-y, but it's *there*, and that's all that matters.

"Hello?" Julian calls again. "Whoever it was talking just now, please respond if you can hear me. This is Pilot-Sergeant Julian Potts from SCV *Surnia*, calling anyone within range of my signal."

*"See, Lyn? I told you there was someone else—fine, fine— Well, I can hear him, at any rate..."* The Florivan voice is more distinct now; the person on the other end of it must have done something to clear up the signal. They seem to be talking to someone else, though, whose voice doesn't carry over Julian's headset. *"Say something else, Sergeant,*

*will you? My counterpart doesn't think you're real."*

"I'm real!" Julian says, stifling a chuckle. "And it's a huge relief that anyone can hear me over this rig at all. Who is this?"

*"Aqua Neyril of LSRV Bee,"* the Florivan voice answers. *"My counterpart is Ranger Captain Marilyn O'Connor—who's pretty irritated with me for chatting with a Fleet pilot when I'm supposed to be listening to her points for the jump we just started."* A clear bell-like giggle accompanies the statement. *"How are you on our channel while we're in the Strange, anyway? I can't say I've ever heard of that being possible even for the non-encrypted nav comm systems civilian ships use."*

Wyndi makes an interested little squeak at all the sounds coming out of his headset and reaches their upper set of hands up to anchor themself by his ear where they can listen. They've been in the habit of doing this for a few months now. Julian's not sure if they understand anything or if it's just curiosity about the sounds, though.

"To tell you the truth, Aqua? I have no idea how or why the rig I'm using works. All I know is that I'm out in the void playing relay buoy trying to get a connection through to any jumper who might be nearby without anyone overhearing—and by some miracle, that's you."

*"Well, Sergeant, you've got your jumper on the line now! Your voice is clearer than I'd expect for a pilot, too. You're quite easy to anchor onto."*

"I'm cross-training for Nav—but that's beside the point. I need your help." Julian counts it doubly as a miracle that he's managed to get through to a Ranger ship.

*"Obviously, if you're reaching all the way into the Strange to*

*talk to me. What's the trouble?"*

"I'm with a stranded ship whose Navigator urgently needs to talk to one of your Elders and we can't use the regular relays ourselves because we're under radio-silence orders. That's why I'm out here on this farm-rigged system in the first place."

*"I'm not an Elder, but we'll be glad to help you—anyone in particular you're trying to reach?"*

"I was told to ask for an Azul with LSS *Caleana Major*, but if you can't get them then any Elder at all is fine."

*"All right, then."* Aqua pauses, presumably to listen to something their counterpart is saying. *"Yes, Lyn, that should work—I won't have any problems taking us halfway out once you're ready."* After another moment or two of silence, the Florivan Ranger is talking to Julian again. *"Okay, Sergeant, can you patch me through to your Navigator? I'll talk to him while Lyn gets on the relays to connect the other end."*

"Great! Thanks, both of you!"

Elias has been staring at the readouts on his reworked pocket-com's holoscreen ever since he turned the system on. He has a chair pulled up on the other side of Dons' little blanket nest from where Li is perched. It's been hours since the First Squadron returned from their maneuvers and conveniently "lost" Sarge. The two of them have been waiting in near silence all this time. Li gets quiet and broody when he's worried, and Elias has been too focused on willing his farm-rigging to work to strike up a conversation himself.

Finally, Elias sees a promising blip on one of the readouts for one of the Quantum Space-filtered channels he's set the darter system up to tap into. A few minutes later, his headset crackles to life.

*"Rudy! Good news!"* Sarge's voice is overlaid with a touch of distortion from the scramble matrix, but it's still understandable. *"I've gotten through to a Ranger and none of your farm-rigging has caught on fire yet."*

Elias flips down his microphone bar and nods to Li. "That's bloody *stellar*, Sarge. Put them through like I showed you. Remember, you'll be out of contact with us yourself while we're on the line with them, even though you'll be hearing everything. If trouble shows up, you'll have to break the connection to warn us."

*"I remember. Good luck—"*

The crackle of all of the relay crystals realigning themselves cuts the pilot's voice off altogether. In a moment, Sarge is replaced by a lightly accented Florivan voice.

*"Hello, there! This is Aqua Neyril from LSRV Bee—my counterpart is seeking out Elder Azul's ship, but I'm here now if I can help."*

Li flips down his own microphone bar and nods back to Elias. "Hello, Aqua. This is Lt. Hsu Li of SCV *Aegolius*, Navigator to Elder Celadon Toreval. Can you hear me?"

*"Ah! Yes, I can! You're downright crystalline—brighter than any human I've ever heard aside from my Lyn, actually. What's the problem?"*

"Short version? My counterpart has been in torpor for a week now from... what do I call it, 'Elder's business'? ...and none of the Fleet's other jumpers are in a position to help at the moment."

*"Stars! No wonder the Sergeant said you were stranded! We might be close enough to lend you a hand or three, actually. It'll take Lyn a bit longer to get Elder Azul on the relays for you, since I'm having to hold us halfway in the Strange to keep*

*this connection while she does that. Can you tell me where you are?"*

"What was your jump-in point?"

*"393 by 1C and 19D."*

"Okay. And your origin star?"

*"Proxima Centauri, heading to Kapteyn."*

Li talks through the rest of the Navigator's orientation points with Aqua, then closes his eyes and starts vaguely gesturing with his left hand. He always does that when he's sorting through his mental index of star charts and calculating hexadecimal location marks with them. Elias has been amazed by that ability of his ever since he first found out about it. Even among Navigators, there's not many who can do what Li can.

"Okay. In that case... ah! We're at 5A3 by 22 and A1, along your current field. That'd be about a week out from you, I think, assuming you run single-skips on standard jump cycles."

*"Bee's a Ranger ship. We can be there in three days, if you need us—maybe less, if we can keep this com setup so I can use both you and Lyn as anchors. Your voice is bright enough... oh! That's why—you're Elder Celadon's Navigator. That makes you the Beacon the Eldest adopted, aren't you?"*

"It does." Li stifles something akin to an embarrassed laugh.

Elias doesn't understand what all the talk of him being a Beacon actually means, aside that Li tends to get adorably flustered whenever it comes up in conversation. The other Florivans he knows refer to it occasionally when they're talking to or about Li, but no one has ever bothered to explain the significance of it to Elias.

*"You should have led with that, Cousin!"* Aqua teases cheerfully. *"I'm from Elder Caeruleus' line—"* They break off mid-sentence, seemingly listening to something that can't be heard over the modified headsets. *"All right, Lyn, I'll tell them—So, we've managed to catch Caleana Major on the Civilian Emergency relay band! Turns out they're making the Proxima-Sol run, so it didn't take as long as Lyn thought it would to connect everything."*

"Thank you, Aqua," Li says, "and pass my thanks to your counterpart as well."

*"Don't mention it, Cousin Li! I'm glad the Strange put us in a place to help. Now, Lyn and I will try not to eavesdrop too much, but we'll have to stay on the line to keep this farm-rigged com relay going. Don't worry, Nida's made sure she's familiar with Elders' business; you don't have to watch your words."*

"Understood."

In a few moments, another click sounds and then a different Florivan is speaking over their headsets. Elias sees a matching set of blips on his readouts—so far, his admittedly rushed system overhaul seems to be holding. In the back of his mind, the thought registers that it might be possible to develop the rigging into something that would be *useful*, but the situation at hand has him too distracted to consider it.

*"Hello? Someone is trying to reach an Elder?"*

Li lets out an audible sigh of relief. "Azul, old friend, you have no idea how good it is to hear your voice."

*"Ah! Sunshine! We've all been missing you and Donnie lately—what's wrong?"*

"A lot of things, right now..." Li starts absently stroking

Dons' ears again while he explains the situation to the Elder.

*"I see what you mean, Sunshine,"* Elder Azul says when he's done. *"You were right to call me. You'll need a medical supply kit—and do you have a set of eye-shields on hand? Analysis specs would be better. Something to shade your eyes."*

"I can get some. Why?"

Elias pats around in his vest pockets. Luckily, Potts' fuzzy little tech thief hasn't gotten those misplaced today. He's surprised by that. Somewhere over on *Surnia*, the kitten must have a dozen pairs of his analysis specs stashed away by now. He wordlessly hands the set of green-lensed glasses over to Li.

Li nods his thanks.

*"You're going to need to seal the room to examine them. Even if it's been a full week, Donnie'll more than likely still have a bit of the Strange left in their brood pouch for the kittens. I know the Eldest made certain you could withstand a touch of miasma, but you'll need to protect your eyes in case they start flickering."*

"We've had our quarters sealed since Celadon first came out of the Drive Bay, but I'll put an extra layer of seals on." Li grimaces. "I really wish y'all believed in telling people how to handle things like this ahead of time, Azul..."

*"If I'd thought Donnie would actually need you to know—"*

"You'd have told me. I know. All right, give me a minute to get the room sealed. Oh, and my..." Li hesitates for a moment and looks over to Elias with a soft sort of a smile. "Well... someone who's very close to me and Celadon is here helping. He's keeping the com link working for me right now, but I don't think we have a second set of specs."

*"Is this the warm fellow Donnie's told me so much about that you might be keeping?"*

Li almost laughs. "I wouldn't be surprised if that's how they described him. But yes."

*"Have him put on a thick blindfold and stay in the room with you, then. You will need a pair of warm hands available, if this is anything like what happened with their last litter."*

Elias raises an eyebrow at Li, hearing all of that. He has no idea what the two of them are talking about anymore.

Li just shakes his head and pulls off the scarf he's wearing, passing it over to Elias and gesturing for him to tie it on while he goes over to close the door. With a few taps on the access pad to the room's computer control system, the shutter on the viewport behind Dons' blanket nest slides closed. Elias hears a subtle shift in the motors of the air circulation system as the last of the vents shut as well to isolate the room fully.

Elias has to take his own headset off to get the makeshift blindfold to stay in place. Without the headset, he can't hear what the Elder is saying to Li anymore. He only hopes that the com link holds, since he won't be able to see to monitor it. Thankfully, he's programmed in a whole set of alert sounds to let him know if something needs his attention.

"All right, Azul. I'm ready. Where do we start?"

A long silence follows, and then Elias thinks he sees a flash of purple-orange light somewhere beyond his covered eyes. The light smells like salt and roses, sending little sparks of lightning across the blindfold's darkness every time he takes a breath. It's not particularly unpleasant, compared to the sort of vertigo he gets from shuttle flight, but the sensation is certainly odd.

"Yeah, you were right... It's not very much miasma, but I'm glad we didn't let anyone else examine them before now... yes, I see them... *Stars*, Azul, *yes*, bleeding, thanks for *that* timely warning... Now tell me what I'm looking at." Li goes into another long silence, listening to whatever it is the Elder is trying to explain to him.

Elias is glad, in a way, that he can't see what's going on or hear the descriptions. He'd never admit it to anyone, but he's always been a bit squeamish when it comes to blood and guts and the like, human or otherwise. The idea of having to watch while whatever is happening to his best friend goes on and listen to the minute details of their private anatomy being explained is thoroughly unappealing. Somewhere in the back of his mind, he remembers that Sarge is off in the void in his darter and *is* having to overhear Elder Azul's instructions. He has a feeling the pilot isn't going to forgive him for that anytime soon; Sarge is pretty easy to gross out, too.

Some time later, he hears the rustle of fabric as Li comes over close to him. "Elias," he says, softly, "I need you to hold something for me."

"Sure."

Elias feels Li's cool, slightly damp hands repositioning his own. He feels his fingers interlaced and then placed together against him right where his vest and shirt are open, leaving a small air pocket between his cupped hands and chest.

"Be very still and stay just like this, okay?"

"Got it."

A few moments pass, and then Li's hands return. They

gently deposit what feels like two thumb-sized masses of fluff in the little cave Elias' fingers are forming. He feels a small rustling movement under his hands as Li leaves him again. Both of the fluffs seem to nestle up against him, and after a moment he feels the tiniest of vibrations coming from each of them. The smell of the air changes, and the notes of lightning on the edges of his closed eyes fade away.

"Are these...?"

"Yeah," Li's voice says from across the room. "Just be gentle and warm. You're good at that."

Slowly, gradually, Toreval starts to slip back out of the warm dreamless darkness they've been floating in.

They're not immediately aware of everything around them, nor able to move enough to even open their eyes. Coming out of torpor takes time, as each small part of their body has to wake up and remember how to move and exist again. That includes their mind, which is slow to come out of the darkness and organize itself into thoughts and memories.

The first sensation Toreval recognizes is that of kittens latched onto the inner lining fur of their brood pouch, coupled with the familiar residual ache from having their insides poked and prodded and rearranged. It hurts more than they remembered, this time, but the soft vibration of their kittens purring supersedes the pain. There's two of them: the precious gifts of the Strange, theirs to raise and protect.

The second sensation is a smell. It's floral and bright like jasmine and citrus and it's floating softly in the air all around them. Toreval knows that fragrance—it's their Navigator's little white wind orchids in bloom. They have a dim recollection of small white buds on the spiked green plant that lives in their bedchamber, what seems like an age ago.

There's a third sensation, too—the feeling of *warmth* beside them soaking into their body wherever it touches.

After a few minutes, as they start to be able to feel and move their ears again, they recognize voices somewhere near them.

"Really, ma'am, what else was I supposed to do?" The first voice is richly accented and *warm* and familiar like the smell of coffee: Elias Rudolph, and in one of his more stubborn moods.

"You disobeyed at *least* six different direct orders, Mr. Rudolph—and that's just the first thing on my list of potential charges to bring against you. How am I supposed to address that, even if your crazy plan *did* work?" The second voice belongs to Jenny Marvin: all smooth, firm green tones like a particularly exasperated river.

"Hey, now! We're *not* all dead in a Novan attack and we've got a bloody *Ranger* ship docking to help us get back to the Fleet—and Dons is alive." Elias punctuates the statement with a charming laugh. "Punish me all you want, ma'am, but I'm going to call this one a win."

"You're *lucky* it worked, mister. That's all I'm going to say."

"Ma'am. Elias. *Please.* If you're going to keep arguing, could you at least go out into the other room to do it?" The sound of leaf-black silk under bright sunlight, speaking softly—that's their Navigator.

Toreval has recovered enough mastery of their body now to open their third eye and look for Li, following the sound of his voice. He's sitting in the nest of their blankets right beside them, the source of the warmth that's helping them to come out of torpor so easily, just like he was when they woke up from almost being frozen—however long ago that even was.

Li's not immediately looking down at them, though, this time. He's too focused on the other two humans he's shooing out of the room.

Toreval finds the strength to reach one of their upper hands over the inch or two they need to rest it on his leg.

Li looks down, almost jumping from the touch. His eyes meet their open one with elation.

"Toreval!" He leans down to wrap his arms around them in an unexpected but gentle and very welcome hug.

"Hello, Navigator... I wasn't asleep that long, was I?" Toreval finds their voice is hoarse from disuse. They can barely manage a whisper.

"Ten days, now. If you ever scare me like that again, I'll..." Li sighs, shaking his head. "You have no idea how worried I was, Val. I thought we were going to lose you."

His dark eyes look wet, they notice, as their gaze falls over the contours of his familiar alien face for the first time in what feels like an eternity. Toreval finds the rest of the strength in their upper pair of arms is returning enough to hug him back.

"No need to worry now," Toreval tells him, still whispering, "I'm fine, see?"

"Val. I had to call Azul."

Toreval recognizes immediately what he's meaning. A flash of grief stabs at them, when the implication sinks in.

"...Happened again, did it?"

"Yeah. I'm sorry, Val... I was able to save the two that had managed to hatch—Elias held them for you while I removed the ones that got caught and didn't make it."

"...How many?"

"Just two. I have them in a stasis box for you. Azul said you'd want to hold them before they were returned to the Strange." Li is still holding them close as he says this, and lightly strokes his hand through their hair. The gesture is a welcome comfort.

"...Thank you."

A long, silent moment passes, while Toreval soaks up his warmth and tries to let their still-vague mind process the reality they've awakened to.

Footsteps coming from the other room catch their attention.

"Did you say something, Li?—Dons! You're awake!" The warm voice of their other favorite human returns as he comes over and stands by the side of their nest at Li's shoulder.

Toreval smiles up at him, still reluctant to let go of their Navigator. "Good morning, Elias," they say, still in a hoarse whisper. "Did I miss anything?"

"Did he tell you you've been out for a week and a half?"

"...Yes. Also that you helped save my kittens. Thank you."

"No need for thanks." Elias reaches over Li and gives one of their free hands a little squeeze. "Just don't go scaring us all like that again any time soon, okay? Li almost gave himself an ulcer worrying about you."

"...Is that right?" Toreval gives his hand a weak squeeze in return. It's just as warm and comforting as always. They don't particularly want to let go.

"Hey!" Li lets go of them now to poke the other man in the ribs. "I wasn't that bad."

"I had to remind you to eat, Li."

"...Oh, is that all?" Toreval yawns and stretches the rest of their arms a little now that more of their body is waking up, still feeling stiff from all the time they've spent in torpor. "I have to do that for him all the time."

"Heh! I'm not surprised." Elias shakes his head. "Glad to have you back with us, Dons."

Toreval finally opens the rest of their eyes and looks closely between their two favorite humans. It's nice to wake up to both of them. They're glad their Navigator hasn't had to be alone through his side of what's happened. A thought flits through the back of their mind from the last conversation they remember clearly. They find enough strength to form a small smirk.

"So, Elias," Toreval asks, now working on stretching their lower arms and tail to get their circulation back, "did you have a chance to ask him yet, or are we still waiting?"

It takes a moment, since for them that conversation was only a few hours ago, while for Elias it's been more than a week, but then he seems to register what they mean. "Oh! Heh." Elias rubs the back of his neck with one hand and replies with a sheepish sort of a smile. "No, hasn't really been a good time... besides, I didn't think it'd be right to ask while he was busy worrying over you."

"Ask me what?"

"Well, Li, y'see—"

"Good to see you awake, Celadon." Jenny's return from the other room interrupts whatever Elias was about to say.

"Thank you." Toreval finishes stretching out their lower arms and starts on their tail and legs. "Sorry for all the inconvenience, Jenny. I really didn't think this would ever come up—I'd have warned you otherwise."

"Lt. Hsu explained things to me. I'm just glad you've come back to us." Jenny nods to them with visible relief. "*Especially* since you're the only person I know who can make the rest of your household stay out of trouble."

"They can't have been all that bad, can they?"

"Oh, you'd be surprised." She chuckles lightly and shakes her head. "I might as well have security paint your pet mechanic's name above his holding cell, with all he's been up to."

Toreval smiles. "Thank you for not putting him back in the brig, then. I'd rather have him here."

"I haven't *yet*, but that doesn't mean Mr. Rudolph here is off the hook. I've half a mind to give him *and* his accomplices to the Rangers as soon as they're done docking with us." Jenny's tone tells them she's only partly joking.

"Rangers? Accomplices?" Toreval looks over to Elias mid-stretch. "Just what exactly did you do this time?"

"Oh, you know me, Dons, can't stand idle hands... just reconfigured Sarge's darter, that's all."

"And left protective custody, *and* encouraged Sergeant Potts to fly off without orders, *and* disobeyed the radio silence order—"

"Throw away the bloody key if you must, ma'am," Elias quips dramatically. "I'm sure you'll need to free me so I can break the rules for you again sooner or later."

"Not anytime soon, mister." Jenny looks down at Toreval and raises her eyebrows, taking on her most serious tone of voice. "And as for *you*, Commander Celadon—you can consider it an order to not get hurt or ill again for at *least* six months. I don't want your Council of Elders coming after me saying you're being put in too much danger or treated badly, understand? I have enough trouble with them as it is."

Toreval smiles and pauses their stretching to give her a little salute. "Understood, Admiral."

"Good." She nods and recrosses her arms. "You're off-duty for the next two weeks, by the way—the Rangers have volunteered to fill in for you until we reach the rest of the convoy, and assist after that for a week or two if you're still recovering."

"Jenny, really, I'll be fine in a few hours."

"Celadon. *No.* That's what you said after you thawed out, and look where we've ended up. I'm not about to let you keep pushing yourself past your limits—especially since I'll need you at full strength once we're back in action." The concerned but firm tone of voice she's using reminds Toreval *entirely* too much of the reprimands they used to get from Azul when they were too rebellious as an apprentice.

"...Understood, Admiral."

"Besides," she says, gesturing vaguely in the direction of the two men, "while the Lieutenant here will still some have work to do, I have a pair of troublesome stowaways from *Surnia* that I need sharp eyes on until I can give them back to Captain Brentwood so she can discipline them. You have more experience raising children than I do, Celadon. *Surely* you can do something to keep them in line for me?"

Celadon laughs. They see what she's getting at—and the idea of spending their enforced leave time with Elias and Mirawynd's young pilot for company is an appealing one.

"I can try, Jenny."

"Good." She turns to go. "You're the only person I know who's a bigger troublemaker. Hopefully that'll cancel them out."

After they hear the click of the outer door closing, Toreval looks up to Li's amused dark eyes.

"I'm not really that much trouble for you, am I?"

"You have your moments, Val." Li pats their head again briefly and then stands and stretches himself. "But believe me, I'd much rather have you around to cause trouble than not."

Toreval's tail swishes contentedly. "Likewise, Navigator."

"Say," Elias interjects with a cheeky grin, "since you're finally up and moving... hungry?"

Toreval pauses to take stock of their body for a moment, then nods. "*Famished*, actually. How did you know?"

"I live with Wyndi, Dons. I know what they're like after a long nap—and you've been sleeping for more than a bloody week. Besides, I haven't managed to haul your counterpart here to the mess yet today, and I figure *he'll* cooperate if you come with us." Elias gives them both a knowing look.

"We had coffee this morning..." Li rolls his eyes, clearly stifling a laugh.

"You're a bloody wonderful hummingbird, yes," Elias teases, "but I don't think your Nav nectar counts as a meal." He turns back to Toreval. "Now, I believe I gave you a rain check for dinner a while back. Since you seem to be my minder now, care to cash that one in?"

"That would be lovely." Toreval finds their way to the edge of their blanket nest. They swing their legs down slowly, since the feeling still hasn't fully returned to their feet. "Let me have a few minutes to freshen up and we can catch my other charges along the way."

"You'll have to wait a few hours to catch Sarge—the Rangers had to pick him up on their way here. Say, Dons? Think you can have a talk with Wyndi about returning my wire picks once he gets back?" Elias smirks teasingly at Li. "Your Navigator here hasn't been interested in negotiating for me."

"Oh, I can try." Toreval giggles softly. "Mirawynd's still in their shiny-stashing phase, though. I keep telling you there's not much I can do about it."

As Toreval starts to stand up, Li offers them his arm. "Here, let me help?"

They sigh and accept his assistance getting to their feet. They don't want to admit just how wobbly they still are. "Thank you. I should be fine to walk..."

"Val, please. Take your time." Li gives them that look that says he's started worrying again. "I don't want you to re-open anything..."

"I promise, I'll be careful." Toreval gives his arm a squeeze. They close their eyes for a moment to focus on regaining their sense of balance. "Let me lean on you as far as the washroom, then? The hot water helps with shaking off the torpor effects..."

"Of course." Li guides them out of their bedchamber. "If you're not up to going all the way to the mess, that's okay. We can bring some food down for you."

Toreval smiles up at him. "I know, but I do want to go."

"Don't worry, Li," Elias teases from behind them, "if they change their mind about walking, I can carry them the rest of the way. It's been a few days since I had a chance to scandalize the ship's gossips..."

Toreval looks back over their shoulder and twitches their ears at him. "Now, really, Elias, why would anyone be gossiping about my heart's-littermate carrying me? I might have to take you up on that offer just on principle now."

"Anytime, Dons." Elias pauses, raising an eyebrow curiously. "'Heart's-littermate?'"

"Yes. Li didn't tell you?" Toreval stops mid-step to turn to face him. "That was how I planned to spring you from the brig."

Li's free hand settles on their shoulder. "We were both a bit distracted, Val. You can adopt him properly *after* you've had a chance to shower and get some food. Okay?"

Toreval laughs, swishing their tail for emphasis. "Yes, Navigator, I'll be good. I can't do anything formal until Mirawynd and the Rangers get here anyway. But until then, to put it in kitten terms..." They smile up at Elias, setting one of their upper hands on his chest for a moment. "*Mine.* Yes?"

"Of course." Elias leans over and hugs them, albeit very gently and only for a moment. He shoots Li an amused look. "No balcony required?"

"Thankfully, no. I'd say we've had enough drama out of them lately as it is."

Toreval gives their Navigator a light, good-natured nudge in the ribs with one of their lower elbows. "Oh, I'm not *that* dramatic, am I?"

"Val, do you really want an honest answer?"

"...Not especially." Toreval gives him their most innocent look, but it breaks as a twinge from their insides makes them catch their breath. "So, about that shower? I don't think I'm up for standing around like this for much longer..."

"Right. No more distractions." Li lets them lean on him again as he guides them the rest of the way. "You'll call if you need us?"

"I will." Toreval nods, leaning now on the door frame of their little shared washroom. "Think you can find my uniform for me in the meantime?"

"And a sweater to wear over it?" Li raises an eyebrow at them.

"Yes, please," Toreval replies cheerfully. Their Navigator knows them too well.

While they're sitting under the nice warm waterfall of the shower cubicle washing off a week's worth of staleness, the thought crosses Toreval's mind that even though the family they were born into is light-years away and hasn't entirely forgiven them for the way in which they left home, at least these two youngest kittens of theirs will have good humans around them as they grow up.

The family they've found for themself is just as warm and caring.

As long as they have Li by their side—and Elias, too, now—they know things will work out.

**★ The End ★**

# APPENDIX

# Timeline of *Strange Space™ Adventures*

The following timeline lists all of the published *Strange Space™ Adventures* and Short Stories in roughly chronological order. Where stories feature major time skips, they have been placed based on the earliest events of that story.

Short Stories marked with *[1] can be found in *Tales of the Navigators: Volume 1*.

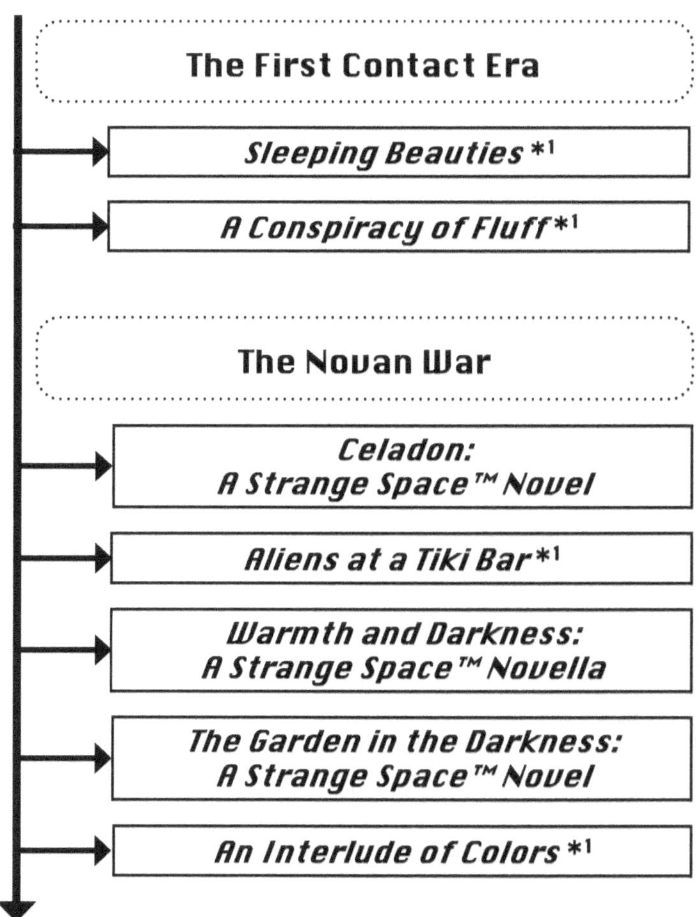

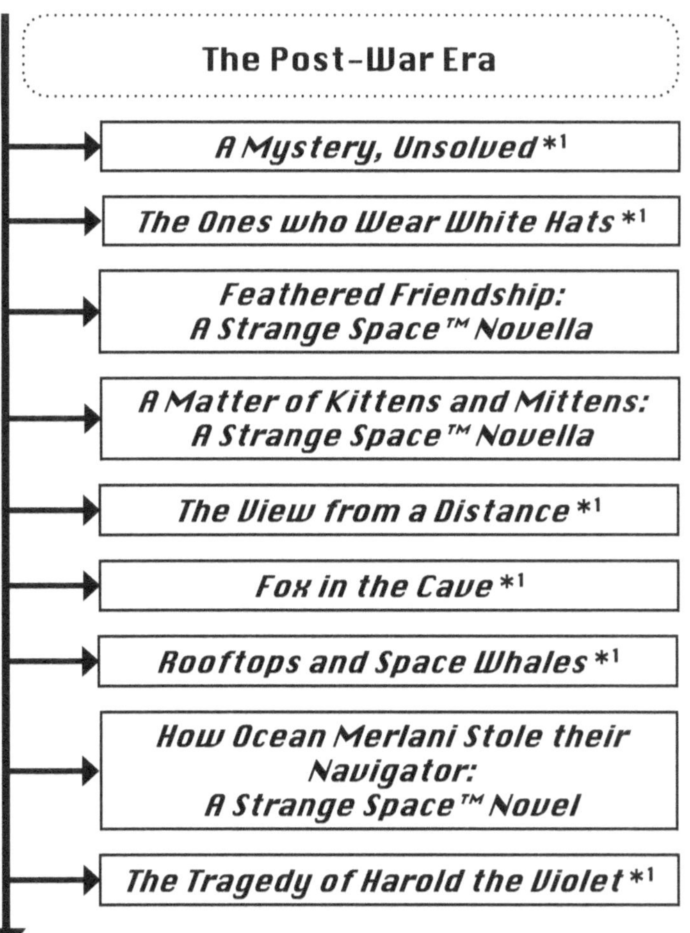

The Post-War Era
A Mystery, Unsolved *1
The Ones who Wear White Hats *1
Feathered Friendship:
A Strange Space™ Novella
A Matter of Kittens and Mittens:
A Strange Space™ Novella
The View from a Distance *1
Fox in the Cave *1
Rooftops and Space Whales *1
How Ocean Merlani Stole their
Navigator:
A Strange Space™ Novel
The Tragedy of Harold the Violet *1

## On the T'irsh-fel

At the beginning of humanity's involvement in the great Novan War, two of the myriad member species of the Greater Galactic Commons introduced themselves directly to Admiral Jennifer Marvin of the Sol Coalition Defense Fleet and her ambassadorial counterparts in the Sol Coalition Diplomatic Corps. These were the T'irsh-fel and the Prelvee, two highly advanced neighbor species who had long been close allies in their common fight against the conquering forces of the Novan Armada. Both allied species had the majority of their resources dedicated to defending their own territory, but worked closely with the Fleet to organize defenses and engagements near the eight star systems of the Sol Coalition.

Much of what is known about the T'irsh-fel is either surface-level or speculative, as they are a somewhat secretive species by nature. One of the definitive facts known is that the T'irsh-fel originated on an ice world similar to modern-day Europa or Earth during the Cryogenian period. As a result of this origin, they tend to colonize similar ice worlds, as they find these more comfortable to live on. T'irsh-fel ships are similarly frigid, and kept at high humidity levels. Likewise, the official Embassy within the Sol Coalition's territory is an extension of the Argadnel Outpost at Europa.

T'irsh-fel individuals who spend large amounts of time in higher-temperature environments are often seen wearing a special form of cooling garment which extends down their back and is anchored to their scales.

The T'irsh-fel themselves are a relatively small-bodied species. An adult individual's thick-scaled, slug-like body is three feet long on average; the scales of their hide vary in size and are bony in composition, with general brown-to-grey coloration. At the 'head end' of the body, a T'irsh-fel sports eight long, stalked appendages, each bearing a single large round eye at its end. The eyes are capable of independent movement, allowing the T'irsh-fel individual a full 360º view of their surroundings at all times. They will often direct several eyes towards one object to bring it into sharper focus as needed. Surrounding the point where the eye stalks connect to the rest of their body, each T'irsh-fel has a thick ruff of long, fluffy "feathers". These structures are brightly colored, usually in reds, oranges, yellows, or purples. T'irsh-fel feathers are poorly understood by humanity's science, although due to their mobility and certain observations made by those who work closely to them, it is suspected that these decorative structures are more akin to the appendages of certain crinoids.

T'irsh-fel are also notable for their telepathic and telekinetic abilities. They are line-of-sight telepathic both with other members of their species and alien life forms. The T'irsh-fel telepathic projection is generally one-way with members of other species, unless a significant personal bond exists with the alien in question. Among other T'irsh-fel, oaths of fealty and bloodline connection often come with a ceremony of telepathic bonding, which allows for direct connection over more significant distances.

Notably for those working with T'irsh-fel allies, the line-of-sight telepathic projection functions over visual communication feeds. Distance does not seem to be a factor, as long as the T'irsh-fel doing the projecting is able to perceive that they are making eye contact with the recipient. While the T'irsh-fel do possess organs analogous to ears and can perceive the spoken words of others, they cannot project their thoughts through audio-only communication media.

The telekinetic abilities of the average T'irsh-fel individual are also based within their immediate line of sight. This ability, however, is not transmissible over visual communication feeds. The strength of the individual's telekinetic abilities is tied to their age and position in the T'irsh-fel social hierarchy. The average T'irsh-fel adult is able to telekineticly lift and manipulate small to medium-sized objects. They can also split their attention between such manipulation and other tasks like movement and telepathic conversation.

While not confirmed, it is suspected that much of the T'irsh-fel's signature technology of manipulable matter is an amplified form of their telekinetic abilities. How they accomplish such wonders as physically merging their shuttlecraft and unmanned fighter drones into the body of their larger starships or moving these ships beyond the light speed barrier is still unknown, as the T'irsh-fel are notoriously secretive about their technology as a whole.

T'irsh-fel social structure and culture is also poorly understood. What is known is that they seem to be strictly hierarchical in their social mindset, and take matters of personal and clan honor very seriously. T'irsh-fel telepathic speech patterns reflect this. When speaking to those outside their own clan group or with whom they have deep personal bonds, the T'irsh-fel always refer to themselves in the third person, usually in the form of "this humble self". They will also tend to call others by their full titles as a sign of respect, and may take it as a deep offense if their own are left off.

As the T'irsh-fel become more closely allied with humanity and the Sol Coalition as a whole, it is hoped that more information about them and their culture will come to light.

## On Florivan Biology and Culture

The Florivans are a curious species by nature.

Roughly humanoid in form with silver-striped blue skin, a second pair of arms below the first, a long tufted prehensile tail, catlike ears at the top of a head crowned with silver hair, and a third golden eye above the first two in the center of the forehead: it's easy to see them both as "human-like" and "entirely alien" all at once.

In the time of *Warmth and Darkness*, the Florivans have been friends with humanity for just over a century. They've been working towards forming a fully integrated society with humanity ever since the exploration vessel LSS *Hulthemia* made first contact with scout ships from Procyon. Florivans had been serving on human starships as part of Astral Navigator/Quantum Space Drive Engineer pairs almost from the beginning of the association between the two species.

Due to a series of devastating epidemics referred to as the "Jungle Plagues" and other events in their history as a species, at this time, the total population of Florivans as a species is in the realm of two hundred thousand adults in total. The majority of these live in the Procyon star system on a planet known as the Sanctuary; roughly one thousand Florivans live at the human colony of Luyten's Star in an area called the North City Sanctuary, and another thousand or so currently serve with the crews of different starships, either as Quantum Space Drive Engineers or apprentices.

Although the Jungle Plagues are mainly to blame for the current "endangered species" status of Florivans, their unusual biology is a core factor in their rarity and the slow rate at which their population can recover from any significant losses.

Florivans reproduce asexually, but only perhaps one in ten of them will ever undergo the metamorphosis to become a reproductive individual. Everything about the process is shrouded in secrecy, as far as humans are concerned. What *is* known, though, by the humans who find themselves as close friends with a Florivan with a reason to tell them, is that even the Florivans themselves cannot control or predict just *who* will undergo the metamorphosis or when it will happen to them.

It's also known that both the metamorphosis itself and the process of going physically into the Strange and "catching" a litter of kittens are potentially deadly. The families of reproductive individuals are very protective of them because of this, as is Florivan society as a whole. To that end, a starship with a reproductive individual as one of its QSD Engineers will *always* have a second Nav/Quan team aboard. (A notable exception to this rule is Elder Celadon Toreval of SCV *Aegolius*, who due to the scarcity of Florivan volunteers in the Fleet and their own medical history, was deemed not subject to the requirement.)

Kittens are caught in litters of two to five, and start

their lives as adorable silver-furred things about the size of a sugar glider. The Florivan parent carries their kittens in a pouch on their abdomen analogous to that of a kangaroo, although they aren't technically marsupials. The kittens grow to about the size of a red squirrel before they begin to mimic words and understand language. As kittens continue to grow, they shed their fur and reveal their unique shade of silver-striped blue skin. Around the same time they shed the last of their fur, Florivan kittens go through a series of growth spurts, after which they are similarly sized to human children and adolescents of the same age.

Occasionally, one kitten out of a litter will be smaller and develop more slowly than their littermates, having a more fragile constitution as a result. Referred to as "survivor-smallest", kittens, those who live long enough to open their eyes tend to take several additional years to grow to maturity. Although few such kittens prove strong enough to survive to adolescence, let alone adulthood, those who do are notable for their higher sensitivity and greater skills in working with Quantum Space. Notably, survivor-smallest kittens never undergo reproductive metamorphosis, but if they do reach adulthood, they are also known to live longer than the average Florivan by several decades.

Adolescent Florivans typically begin their apprenticeships to learn how to work in Quantum Space between the ages of ten and thirteen. The age at which a Florivan is released from their apprenticeship to either join the crew of another starship with their chosen human counterpart or seek additional training in their preferred career specialty depends entirely on the speed at which they mature into the skills their mentor is required to teach them in order to be safe and competent adults. Typically, Florivans are between fifteen and twenty when released from their apprenticeships. Florivans are considered 'adults' around the age of twenty to twenty-five, although they are usually fully grown and considered mature enough to select a human counterpart by age fifteen.

Usually, a Florivan reproductive individual is between thirty-five and fifty Earth-Standard years old at the time of their metamorphosis. On very rare occasions, a Florivan under the age of twenty-five will undergo the metamorphosis; these individuals seldom survive catching their first litter, and the younger they are the less likely it is they will survive the metamorphosis itself. Only one reproductive individual of this type, Celadon Toreval, has ever been known to survive an adolescent metamorphosis and live to be named an Elder of the Council.

Florivan culture, in many ways, has developed around these quirks of their biology. The leaders of Florivan society are the Elders of the Council: reproductive individuals who have survived both the metamorphosis and the catching of their first two litters of kittens. An Elder's littermates, traditionally, become part of their household to assist with their kittens. The Elder's "line" then grows with each of their subsequent litters, as well as other non-reproductive individuals who are adopted into the household over time.

Florivan society is built around family and close friendship, and has always been peaceful—in no small part because they instinctively consider all other members of their species as close kin. A Florivan's human counterpart is considered a member of their family as well, usually along the level of connection as a sibling. Florivan Elders commonly adopt the counterparts of their adult kittens into their households. Traditionally, the compacted Florivan/human pair is treated as a family unit, similar to what humans would call a platonic partnership. Such pairs typically form after the Florivan has finished their QSD Engineer apprenticeship and remain together for life.

Another important aspect of Florivan culture when compared with humanity is their relationship to the very human concepts of gender, sexuality, and romance. To put it bluntly, Florivans by nature have no concept of these things. They are, without exception, genderless, asexual, and aromantic, to use the most accurate human terms.

(Florivans do, of course, find the vast diversity among their human friends fascinating! It's part of why they think humans are neat.)

In light of their genderless nature, Florivans are always referred to with singular "they/them" personal pronouns in English and whatever neutral equivalent is most appropriate in other human languages. They also exclusively use neutral terms such as "Nida" (parent) and "Entile" (parent's sibling) when referring to other members of their family.

## On Character Identities and Pronouns

*Warmth and Darkness* takes place in a far future setting in which human society has long since reached the stage of accepting and celebrating all varieties of diversity. This is a sort of world that I, personally, would like to live in. I don't claim it to be a *perfect* setting, but I do take an optimistic view of our potential as a species.

Several of the human characters presented in this story would, in today's terms, likely identify with one or more communities under the LGBTQIA+ umbrella. While the narrative of this story did not call for the characters to specifically state which labels they would use, and I like to imagine that a lot of who they are can be inferred through their interactions, as a member of the LGBTQIA+ community *myself*, I'm aware of the importance of clear representation. Seeing characters like ourselves in stories where they are valued for who they are and able to live without being marginalized for their nature is, in my opinion, *powerful*, and a big part of my philosophy as a writer.

Please note that at the same time, it is impossible to represent an entire community in the form of one character. My characters are simply themselves, and while they draw on my own experiences and those of people I know, they are not meant to be "perfect" renditions of one thing or another. Just like every human, their various identities are *aspects* of them, rather than the entirety of their personality.

That all being said, the following characters who feature in this story would like to "come out" to you and share this aspect of their lives:

**Admiral Jennifer Marvin** would describe herself as asexual and aromantic.

**Elias Rudolph** would describe himself as homosexual/homoromantic. (In his words: "a man who happens to be attracted to other men." Rudy has never been all that interested in labels of any sort.)

**Lt. Hsu Li** would describe himself as pansexual and demi-romantic.

(Note: Please keep in mind that this is not an exhaustive list of the LGBTQIA+ characters who appear in this story, any more than it is a full description of each of the characters in question. These are simply the ones who feature most prominently and asked me to clarify their identities.)

On behalf of all of my characters, humans and Florivans alike, I'd like to thank you, dear reader, for being accepting of them and respecting their preferred sets of pronouns.

I hope that we all will one day live in a world like the one these characters inhabit, in which a person can openly be themself without fear. I do believe it's possible for us to get there, too; every small step we make in the right direction matters.

—Katie Silverwings

*Katie Silverwings is a glassblower, visual artist, and writer, originally from Texas and now a nomadic creative spirit. She holds a BA in English and History from McMurry University in Abilene, Texas, as well as a BA (Hons.) in Glass from the University for the Creative Arts in the UK. Silverwings identifies as aromantic, asexual, and genderfae; "she/her", "they/them", and "fae/faer" pronouns are all welcome.*

*Long fascinated by nature and space, Silverwings' speculative fiction work centers around notions of optimistic futurism, friendship, found family, and adventurous journeys into the known and unknown. Her characters do most of the driving, and she does her best to keep up and negotiate pleasing stories with them.*

*Silverwings' two cats are commonly found staring over her shoulder while she's writing. The small cloud of dark matter with eyes likes to sit in her lap and interfere with typing, while the calico makes operatic editorial comments from across the room.*



**www.KatieSilverwings.com**

**@KatieSilverwings**

# More Books
# by Katie Silverwings

# Celadon

## ✶ A Strange Space™ Novel ✶

The Novan War has just begun. All that stands between Humanity and utter destruction are the ships of the Sol Coalition Defense Fleet.

The only problem? None of those ships are equipped with the all-important Quantum Space Drive which allows humanity to travel between planets and stars at a reasonable scale of time. The Drive needs Florivan QSD Engineers to run it, and Florivans are pacifists. Their Council of Elders has never allowed service on military vessels.

The Fleet can do little more than sit at the edges of the Coalition's seven member systems and *wait* for the Novans to attack.

Celadon Toreval is the Youngest of the Florivan Council of Elders. If anyone can come to Fleet Admiral Marvin's aid and help her save her people—and theirs—it's them.

Celadon, though, has their own reasons to get involved...

Available now from Amazon and Barnes & Noble and at
## www.KatieSilverwings.com

# Feathered Friendship

# How Ocean Merlani Stole their Navigator

✶ A Strange Space™ Novel ✶

Every starship wanting to use the veiled dimension of Quantum Space as a shortcut around the physical distance between planets and stars needs a Florivan to run the Drive.

Every Florivan QSD Engineer needs an Astral Navigator to orient them and keep them anchored to Normal space. Finding the *right* human to be their life-long counterpart is one of the most important choices a young Florivan ever makes.

What happens, then, to someone like Ocean Merlani Barker, who can't seem to click with *any* of the highly qualified Navigator prospects their instructors have to offer? Ocean themself seems content to spend their second year in the Nav/Quan training program alone and taking extra classes for their secondary degree in geosciences.

Content, that is, until a chance encounter with a certain graduating student from the Security/Tactical program changes the course of their life forever...

# The Garden in the Darkness

www.ingramcontent.com/pod-product-compliance
Lightning Source LLC
Chambersburg PA
CBHW021549310726
48972CB00003B/743